THE HOLY DAYS OF GREGORIO PASOS

A Novel By

RODRIGO RESTREPO MONTOYA

Two Dollar Radio
Books too loud to Ignore

Two Dollar Radio
Books too loud to Ignore

WHO WE ARE TWO DOLLAR RADIO is a family-run outfit dedicated to reaffirming the cultural and artistic spirit of the publishing industry. We aim to do this by presenting bold works of literary merit, each book, individually and collectively, providing a sonic progression that we believe to be too loud to ignore.

TwoDollarRadio.com

Proudly based in
Columbus
OHIO

   @TwoDollarRadio

 @TwoDollarRadio

/TwoDollarRadio

Love the
PLANET?
So do we.

Printed on Rolland Enviro.
This paper contains 100% post-consumer fiber, is manufactured using renewable energy - Biogas and processed chlorine free.

 100%

PCF

 BIO GAS ENERGY

∞ PERMANENT

Printed in Canada

All Rights Reserved

COPYRIGHT → © 2023 BY RODRIGO RESTREPO MONTOYA

ISBN → 9781953387332 : *Library of Congress Control Number available upon request.*

Also available as an Ebook.
E-ISBN → 9781953387349 : **Book Club & Reader Guide** of questions and topics for discussion is available at twodollarradio.com

SOME RECOMMENDED LOCATIONS FOR READING:
Pretty much anywhere because books are portable and the perfect technology!

COVER PHOTOS → TOP: Biodiversity Heritage Library/Flickr; CENTER LEFT: thom masat/Unsplash; CENTER RIGHT: Victor_g/Unsplash; BOTTOM LEFT: Fernanda Fierro/Unsplash; BOTTOM RIGHT: Jakob Owens/Unsplash. **DESIGN** → Eric Obenauf.

ANYTHING ELSE? Yes. Do not copy this book—with the exception of quotes used in critical essays and reviews—without the prior written permission from the copyright holder and publisher. Without limiting the rights under copyright reserved above, no part of this publication may be reproduced, stored or introduced into a retrieval system, or transmitted, in any form or by any means.

WE MUST ALSO POINT OUT THAT THIS IS A WORK OF *FICTION*. Names, characters, places, and incidents are products of the author's lively imagination, or used in a fictitious manner. Any resemblance to real events or persons, living or dead, is entirely coincidental.

We would like to acknowledge that the land where we live and work is the contemporary territory of multiple Indigenous Nations.

"Oh God, I was feeling baptized by the world. I had put a roach's matter into my mouth, and finally performed the tiniest act."

—Clarice Lispector,
The Passion According to G.H.

THE HOLY DAYS OF GREGORIO PASOS

TUCSON

The longer you live the shorter a day becomes. The same goes for a year. I'm on a couch in Tucson and will be for another month. When I got to the hospital, the first thing the nurse asked me was my name. It was difficult to breathe and harder to speak. My sister, Ana, spoke for me. "Gregorio Pasos," she said.

The nurse nodded as he filled out my intake form. He did so in green pen, in a room full of light.

"How old are you?" the nurse asked.

"He's twenty-one," Ana said.

My sister explained. I was playing goalkeeper in a Sunday league soccer game. I dove for a loose ball in the box. The forward slid. I got there first. Both of his cleats landed on my ribs. My body fell limp, face first in the dead grass. "It was like he'd fallen asleep," Ana said.

Ana propped me up against the post. My teammates stood quietly in a circle around us. She held her fingers up and urgently asked me to count them. "Three," I said. "Four." The more time passed, the worse I felt. I described my symptoms. Each breath was accompanied by a sharp pain. I told her I was losing air. Luckily, the hospital was nearby. St. Mary's. Ana drove me.

The nurse asked a lot of questions. The doctor asked fewer. An X-ray was ordered. The result was bad but could've been worse. Four broken ribs and a collapsed lung. The doctor proceeded to insert a long needle between two ribs and drain the excess air. Nothing could be done for the ribs. "They will heal on their own," she said, "in due time." What mattered most was my lung. For it to recover, I would have to breathe normally. Therefore, they prescribed pain pills. When I asked what kind, the nurse laughed. "Some of the strongest we have," he said.

An hour later, the doctor sent me home. She told me to rest. "Take a month off from work, two if you can. Stay home and take it easy, both physically and mentally. Take your medication. Expect your mind to slow. Expect a haze. Expect nausea. Sleep all you need to. Try not to move. Try not to laugh. Eat well, but not too much. If you have any problems, we'll be here."

The hospital bill, thankfully, hasn't arrived.

My first soccer injury happened when I was eleven. I dove for a low cross and was kicked in the face by the other team's forward. I woke up to my father and the taste of copper. We sat together on the sideline. The game had resumed as soon as my father had carried me off. His sleeves were marked with my blood. At the hospital, the doctor had me touch my finger to my nose. First with my left hand, then with my right. Then I was to follow her finger with my eyes. We were at the hospital for less than an hour. I went to school the next day.

I was thirteen when I suffered my second. A through ball was played toward goal. I called off my defender and went out for it, sliding. My defender didn't hear me and kneed me in the mouth. I woke up minutes later, on the field, to my mother. I was on my back and had to squint to see her. I counted her fingers. I lost two teeth. I remember her picking them up from the grass and holding them in her cupped hand as we walked off.

Often, a rattlesnake commits the crime of living on human property. When this happens, certain people call a specialist to have the snake relocated. In Tucson, people call my boss. Then he calls me. I grab the snakes with a special pole and place them into a secure bucket. On average, only half of relocated rattlesnakes survive. The other half die starving. They don't know where to go or what to do. I drive the snakes out to the desert and do my best to find a home for them to learn to live in.

The biggest rattlesnake I've ever moved was the diamondback under Ramona's bed. That's how we met. She'd fallen asleep, in the middle of a Saturday afternoon, with the screen door open to a view of her garden. She'd conducted her research before I'd arrived, about rattlesnake relocation and their chances of survival. She insisted I move the snake back out into the yard.

This morning, Ramona and I watched the sun rise from our bedroom. We ate breakfast and read the same article, side by side. The article was about the planet, the end of food, climate plagues, unbreathable air, poisoned oceans, economic collapse, and perpetual war.

We agreed, once again, not to have children of our own.

"We'll get a cat," I said.

Ramona laughed. "Or a dog."

"Both."

My sister lives down the road and has taken up, of all things, baking. Her latest loaf of seed bread, half of which remains on my kitchen counter, is her best yet. She made it just for me, on account of my injury.

Most of the time, she works. She represents detained, mentally ill immigrants seeking asylum in the United States. Just the other day she won another case. She used to celebrate her victories with bourbon. Now she celebrates with marijuana, pastries, and sweet tea.

We were living on opposite sides of the country when she called me from a mental hospital. Two of her clients had gone missing. She said she was never going to drink again. The doctor had diagnosed her as borderline. She sobbed as she spoke. She called it a curse.

Before ending the call, she asked me to pray. For her and for them. I prayed. A week later, I moved across the country to be with her. To Tucson.

Our father lives alone in Connecticut. He has two black Labrador retrievers, a brother and sister from the same litter. They, too, are recovering. He's been neutered. She's been spayed. They're in stitches with cones around their large block heads.

He calls to ask how I'm feeling. I tell him the truth. It hurts to do anything, and the medication makes me sick. We end up talking about my sister. The same conversation repeats. I say she's good, she's doing better, and that better is great. We go back and forth.

"Like any parent, I will always ask myself what I could have done different," he says.

"She's still alive," I say.

He thinks that he and my mother could've provided more structure. More rules and expectations. Sometimes, when he's most regretful, I tell him what I really think. They could have done better, sure, but if it weren't for them, she would be much worse.

In Colombia, my mother shares an apartment with my grandmother and aunt. One is lost in Alzheimer's. The other's cancer has spread from the ovaries to the pancreas. My mother sleeps with her fists clenched so tight she wakes up with bloody palms. She weeps to me over the phone. "I am praying for them to die," she says. She tells me something else that she's already told me twice before. "When I die, don't be sad," she says, "I will be happy. I will be done."

It's difficult to stand and hard to think. Ramona makes me tea, holy basil, and it helps. A year ago, we went out on our first date. We sat in a tea shop for hours. "Where are you from?" Ramona asked. "Why are you here?" The same question asked two ways. A question, back then, I couldn't quite answer.

My response was straightforward. I said I'd moved to Tucson because of my sister. A simple, incomplete truth. I'd chosen not to explain myself on account of a fear that the whole truth was too strange. Now, I wish I'd told her everything. An ordinary regret. Old, I suppose, as time.

Lost in the fog of my medication, the past comes to me in pieces. I think of my family, Ramona, and a few others. Even now, I still can't answer Ramona's original questions. I try to recall how I got here. To Tucson, to this house, to this couch. This is the best way I can put it now. I know where I am, but I don't know where I've been. There's something I've lost, but I don't know what.

Ramona's lived in Tucson all twenty-five years of her life. Parts of her family have been here for a century. She works as a landscape architect. Lately, she's been busy designing a community garden for the base of Tumamoc Hill, up the road from our home, across the street from St. Mary's Hospital. Originally, Tumamoc was home to the Hohokam. For over two thousand years, it has remained significant to their descendants, the

Tohono O'odham and the Pima. Trincheras, petroglyphs, dwellings, agricultural systems, roads, and burial sites remain. Today, the state university uses Tumamoc for research.

Ramona and I walk to the top a couple of times a week, in the evenings. A statue of the Virgin of Guadalupe stands at the base. Large slabs of mountain stone are regularly graffitied in black. *Native Pride*, they say. The graffities are painted over soon after, only to emerge again days later.

Last night, Ramona and I watched a movie when she got back from work. Tired, we chose something short, quiet, and void of plot. *Rodeo*.

The movie is no more, and no less, than an observation of a persistent American mythology. It's a familiar cast. There's the bull, the cowboy, the sage old man, the clown, the brass band, and a large crowd. Stoic cowboys watch other cowboys get tossed, kicked, and stomped. The main character wears a red shirt. When he rides, the footage slows. A lone violin plays "Amazing Grace." The cowboy falls. The bull bucks violently above him. Finally, he's saved by the clown. The cowboy has failed to qualify. The rodeo continues. The movie ends.

The film reminded us of Ramona's uncle. He, too, rides bulls. I asked if he'd ever gotten hurt.

"More times than you," she said.

"And how's his health?"

"Excellent."

He'll be riding in Tucson in February. Ramona said we should go.

"I've been to a bullfight," I said, "but never a rodeo."

She laughed. "It'll be your first."

From the couch where I sit, I can see two mourning doves mating on the fattest branch of a palo verde. They had been perched together, still and in peace, before joining suddenly in a wild hurry. Then they disappeared. First one, then the other. Yesterday, a dove flew into the window and died. This is common. As common as two doves mating.

PART ONE

DANBURY

I was living where I'd been born, in a town named Danbury, in a house for sale. I was eighteen and on the verge of graduating. Soccer season had just ended, in the quarterfinals, in the rain. The game had gone to penalties. I didn't save one. I was born with flat feet and the habit of guessing. That night I guessed wrong. Nobody had blamed me and neither had I. Still, I wept. Weeping is another habit of mine. I've had it since birth.

In April I mailed a love letter to Ms. Monti, the Spanish teacher. Latin American Literature was my best class, my only good one. Spanish was Ms. Monti's second language, my first. She wouldn't let me grade but did let me make copies and choose stories and movies for her to teach. When I would talk to her about my life, she would always listen. The letter stated that I was drinking wine and proposed that she and I get together and do the same. I left it in her mailbox at school. The principal called me into his office the next day. He explained that he had to do his job and suspend me for a week. I didn't know what to say. I said nothing. He went on to apologize for the whole situation. He'd heard I hadn't taken the end of the soccer season well, and he was aware that I hadn't been thriving academically. I think he was more uncomfortable than I was. I felt bad for him. I did my best to say something that would make him feel better. "We're all adults here," I said, "I understand."

Ana was already living and lawyering in Tucson. Her drinking was bad and was only getting worse. My mother was preparing for a divorce and my father was doing the same. The house was warm and clean. The market was good, the realtor was around, and I was in the way.

My uncle Nico lived alone and my parents thought it would make sense for me to stay with him for a little while. Nico was sick and his days were numbered. "You'll take good care of each other," they said. They were right. It was May and the days were long. I went.

GOLD, WATER, BLOOD

The last time I'd seen Nico had been Christmas. He'd been his usual self. Discreet, drunk, and observant. I'd gone up to bed before the conversation had wandered offshore and into banter. Nico and my father had remained by the fire until morning. I'd fallen asleep upstairs to the dim sound of their drinking. I woke up to a different noise. Laughter and some weeping.

According to my parents, Nico and I had been born very much alike. They said so several times throughout my childhood and adolescence. My father liked to say Nico and I were both muted. My mother said we were remote. Whenever the subject of our similarity came up, Nico would look at me and shrug. He did so with a combination of amusement and lament. I trusted my parents' assessment as much as I did Nico's reaction. I didn't have anything to add, so I laughed along with them.

Nico lived two towns over in a square two-bedroom house. I arrived in the middle of the afternoon and knocked on the front door. A fallen tree was rotting in the yard and the weeds looked like flowers. Nico had lost weight and his black hair was beginning to thin evenly on all sides of his narrow head. His eyes had grown as yellow as his teeth. Regardless, he smiled.

"You look good," I said.

"Gregorio," he laughed, "you're late for lunch."

Nico ate slowly. He spread the beans over his rice and cut into his steak. "The fat," he said, "is the best part." I finished my plate in minutes. Then I served myself another. I had two plates in the time it took Nico to eat half of his. Once we'd finished eating, he scraped what was left into his black cat's bowl. "Tuesday," he called. Tuesday continued lying on the couch. She opened her eyes, looked at Nico, then returned to sleep. Nico started a cigarette and set his pack down on the table. He told me to take one and I did. We talked about soccer. He reminisced about his playing days. He'd been a target forward and had been especially good in the air, with his head. I told Nico the story about the many times my father stood behind the goal I was tending to during any one of my team's matches, how he would smoke his cigarette and tell me to kick it farther. As if I could.

Nico asked if I'd heard from my sister. I hadn't. We got through the subject of my parents' divorce almost as quickly. All Nico asked me was how I felt.

"I think the divorce is a good idea," I said.

Nico nodded. "But how do you feel?" he asked.

"Good," I said.

Nico showed me to my temporary room. There was a twin bed in the corner and a filing cabinet that doubled as a dresser. The only decoration was a framed photo mounted on the wall of two black stone sculptures, two fat doves. One stood round and intact with its eyes open and forward. The other dove was cracked through its chest and talons, blown apart.

"What's up with these?" I asked.

Nico pulled two glasses from the cupboard and a bottle of rum from the freezer. We sat at the kitchen table and opened the window beside us to hear the crickets sing. I took a sip of the straight rum and pretended to like it. Nico laughed. I would've been embarrassed if it hadn't been just us.

"Do you want the short version or the long one?" he asked.

"The long one."

"If you say so," he said. "I was living in Medellín at the time. Where I was born. Your father was away at university in Bogotá. He had a good life there. He lived in a small apartment downtown, halfway between two universities. In the mornings, he attended one. In the evenings, he attended the other. He spent his free time pursuing your mother. She didn't want anything to do with him at first. He sent her poems. Some original, some plagiarized. He called her house daily and struck up a strategic friendship with his future mother-in-law, running errands for her and helping out around the house. Eventually, your mother gave your father a chance. Your father has told you these things, hasn't he?"

I nodded. "At least four or five times," I said.

Nico laughed. "Anyway, I was living with your grandfather and sleeping in the same twin bed I'd always slept in, next to an identical bunk that had once been your father's. I remember it well, lying awake, alone with all of our family's ghosts. I'd bring it up to your grandfather in the morning, over coffee. He'd answer calmly, as if he too had been lying awake at night, next to me, with nothing but a wall between us. He knew. *The ghosts were here first*, he'd say."

"Ghosts?" I asked.

Nico sat himself up in his chair. "Both my mother and my sister had already died. My mother had a stroke when I was eleven; my sister committed suicide when I was sixteen." Nico's voice trailed off. He shook his head, shrugged, then shook his head again. I knew better than to ask for an explanation. I waited for him to speak. Nico reached for the rum, then for a cigarette, and kept on with his story.

"Anyway. I went to university, too, but left after about a month of classes. My girlfriend Violeta had convinced me to enroll, but she couldn't convince me to stay. As they say, it wasn't for me. With Violeta and her mother's help I found work at the Museo of Antioquia, in Medellín, where most of Botero's paintings and sculptures were displayed. I did whatever was asked of me. I sold tickets, I made coffee, I answered phones. I even did some cleaning. Believe it or not, the cleaning was my favorite part. When I cleaned, I was all alone with the sculptures and the paintings in the yellow light of the silent museum. I felt at home, surrounded by portraits of the people I'd always known. The rich, the poor, and the good. There, I learned how to be. I mopped the tile floors. I left the bathrooms spotless. There's no better feeling than leaving a place cleaner than you found it. I was where I belonged. I was useful. Once, Botero attended an event at the museum. A fundraiser, I believe, or a gallery opening. I don't remember which. It went late into the night. I began cleaning, despite the party. Botero was one of the last to leave. As he walked out, he thanked me."

"What did you say?" I asked.

"I thanked him, too."

Nico left for the bathroom. When he came back, five minutes or so later, he stumbled into his chair. It seemed as if he'd been crying.

"The job helped me save some money. At the time, I didn't exactly know what for. I was saving money for the same reasons anyone saves money. In case my father lost his job or became sick. In case Violeta and I married or had children. I saved what felt like a lot of money at the time. It was a lot. It was enough."

"Enough for what?" I asked.

Nico coughed, tried to speak, then coughed again.

"To leave," Nico said. "To leave. I don't know if you can comprehend it. It's not something you, you who grew up here with what you've had, can ever really understand, even if you really wanted to. Every time I left the house, I didn't know if I would make it back home. Every time your grandfather left the house, every time I got off the phone with your father, I knew it could be the last time we'd ever speak. The same was true with Violeta. I worried about everyone I knew, and especially everyone I loved. There were bombs on buses, planes, office buildings, supermarkets. I knew people who, upon hearing an explosion, looked out their window and saw the burning remains of a car raining onto their lawns. I've seen these pieces of burned metal in people's homes. People killed people because. Dead politicians. Dead journalists. Dead activists. Peaceful people, dead. Dead parents, dead children. People here, in America, they've asked me questions. They've said, *Hey, Nico, don't you miss Colombia?* The answer is yes. Of course I do. I have missed Colombia my entire life."

Nico filled our glasses with ice and rum. The cubes cracked as he poured.

"To be Colombian is an act of faith. Nothing more. For many people, that is enough. Most people have no choice. You don't know how little a person can have. I don't either, but I've seen it. I've met them. I've met their children. I've known their names. In Colombia, hungry parents give their children English names in hopes that someday their children will land ashore a place where they can be happy. They name their children after Catholic saints and Spanish priests. That's what happens. Here, I live a life in broken English. Today, all I have to say is hello, goodbye, and good luck. That's how I stay silent. I have myself to talk to. I have you too, I guess."

"What about the doves?" I asked.

"The doves," Nico said. "Originally, there was only one sculpture. A Botero. He'd donated it to the city of Medellín and they put it in a plaza, in Parque San Antonio. Years later, the city held a festival there. My girlfriend, Violeta, invited me to go with her and some friends, but I stayed home. One of the cartels had installed a bomb behind the dove statue, beneath the feathers that stuck out from its backside. It killed more than thirty people. Violeta was one of them. Had I been there, I would've died too. Sometimes I wish I'd gone with her. I left Colombia a week later. They asked Botero to replace the dove. He told them to leave it there. He built another one and made sure it was installed alongside the original. That's why there's two."

"You left a week later?" I asked.

"I left a week later. I wrote my father and brother a letter once I had an address here in the States. I can only imagine what they must've thought had happened to me. They must've assumed the worst. I should've written the letter sooner. But that's always the trouble with letters, isn't it? I told them I loved them and that I was sorry. Every now and then I think about what I wrote, why I did what I did and said what I said, why I left without telling them. If there's anything you learn from me, and I hope it's not much, it's this. There is only one kind of letter. A love letter. To write a real one, you have to be sorry."

"Nico," I said.

"I've said too much. I'll finish this story and we'll leave it at that. A month later I received a letter from your grandfather. I still have it. I read it when I need to. It's very short. I could show it to you, but I know it by heart. *Beloved Nico, I'm not angry you left without a word. I'm not angry at all. What matters is that you're safe. What matters is that you're good.*"

SCHOOL DAYS

There was a month of school left and attendance for graduating seniors was optional. Nico couldn't have cared less whether I went or not. I think he would've preferred it if I'd stayed with him while he read through newspaper after newspaper in the morning, if I'd helped him with his crosswords, if I'd been there for us to dissect daytime television together. He never went so far as to try to keep me from going. He had the habit of pouring me a drink or two every evening, be it a Monday or a Thursday, then asking me if I had plans the next morning, knowing full well I had class. In return, I'd ask him what his plans for the next day were, knowing full well he never did much of anything. "Tomorrow I'm taking the day off," he'd say. My father supported Nico financially. He'd done so for decades. I suppose, in some way, Nico had earned it.

Despite my failed romance with Ms. Monti, we remained friends. She told me about the boyfriend she'd had for eight years who never proposed. About her absent father and difficult mother. About standardized testing and her performance review. The Master's Administration Degree she was slowly finishing up, night class by night class, and the book she wanted to write about her imprisoned uncle. One morning, I kept her company during her free period. I was helping her make copies to prepare for her next lesson. The phone rang. She answered. She screamed. "My mother died," she said, then ran out of the classroom. I knew there was nothing I could do. I went to the library and took a seat on one of the couches. The principal came and told me that he'd spoken with Ms. Monti. He asked me if I was okay. I asked him if Ms. Monti was okay. He shook his head. I stayed in the library for a few hours. At one point the frontrunner for valedictorian took a seat on the couch next to mine. He did most of the talking, mostly about his Ivy League future and his growing interest in robotics. I don't know why I didn't leave. He questioned the value of literature, the value of good books. He dared me to change his mind. Somehow, I'd inherited a debate. Naturally, I lost.

I had a few friends. Sometimes we got high and drove around. Eventually, we'd buy some sandwiches at the deli and go to the bridge, where my friends would do backflips into the lake. Afraid, I preferred to stay ashore and watch. The day the Spanish teacher's mother died, we got on the tired subject of our futures. When questioned about my plans, I said that I was going to sell my blood, my plasma, and maybe even a kidney.

I got especially high that day. Too high to drive. One of the other guys volunteered to take the wheel until I regained direction. We were on our way to the gas station for tobacco and rolling papers when the driver misread a sharp turn and drove us into a tree. The driver was the first to get out. The two guys in the back quickly followed. I remained there, in the passenger seat of Nico's totaled car. I was slow to get out. It was like I was trying to wake up from a dream except there was no dream. My friends pulled me out through the window. I was completely unharmed, like nothing had happened.

That night I explained myself to my parents. I told them the truth about Ms. Monti's mother and a lie about the family of deer appearing in the middle of the road. I don't know if they believed anything I said. The primary takeaway was that everyone was okay. We talked for a while over dinner. I mentioned the history Nico had told me some weeks before. I explained to them what I'd learned. How easy it was to die in Colombia and how little one could do about it. On the other hand, how strange it was to live in a town where people's biggest threats seemed to be themselves. My parents thought it would be best if I stayed the night at home. I talked my way into getting a ride to Nico's. When I got there, he was at the kitchen table, rum in hand. "Sit down," he said.

I got lucky. Nico was able to buy an older model of the same car. He let me keep driving. He let me stay.

WHITE MICE

Tuesday was a good cat. Tuesday was tired. Tuesday was dying. Days after I moved in, she began to keep to herself. She had no interest in food. She spent her last days beneath Nico's bed-frame, in hiding, approaching death with an instinctual desire for solitude. Nico told me all about Tuesday's good life one Saturday afternoon. I was supposed to get together with some friends of mine. For the hundredth time, we had big plans to get drunk and stoke a bonfire in the woods. I had little interest in staring at a fire and even less in listening to someone learn to play a guitar. What I wanted was to be with Nico, and Tuesday.

"I've never been one to keep people from leaving," Nico said, "and I've never been any different with Tuesday. She was no more than a kitten, the equivalent of a teenager, when I first found her. She was sifting through my garbage can next to the garage. I fed her every day for a week and finally she followed me into the house and stayed the night. She liked to tap on the window and look back at me. It was her way of asking to go. I was afraid to let out her at first, but eventually I accepted the fact that I wasn't her mother. We reached an agreement. A silent one, but an agreement, nonetheless. I'd let her go so long as she would come back. Tuesday always returned with gifts. She started with easy prey. Crickets. Roaches. Fallen birds. As she got older, she brought white mice. It was her way of thanking me. She never toyed with the mice. She never ate them, either. Every time she returned, I'd open the window and greet her. She'd walk in, slowly, head up, her eyes on mine, and she'd drop the mouse in my open hand. A few months ago, Tuesday began eating less. She got slower. She slept more. I'd still let her out when she asked, but she'd come home empty handed, and sorry. *It's okay*, I'd tell her, *I understand*. I don't let her out anymore. She doesn't ask. All she can do is sleep. Tuesday does her best to hide her pain from me, the way the smartest animals do, but I see it clearly now. I know her too well. It's time for her to sleep for good. I owe it to her."

Tuesday refused the sedatives. "Hold still," Nico whispered. He kissed the top of Tuesday's head and looked into her gold eyes. Nico's trembling hands moved slowly over Tuesday's ribs. He waved me over to the kitchen tile and told me what to do.

"When I open Tuesday's mouth, I need you to make sure she swallows the pills. Drop them in the back of her throat. Once she's swallowed those, do the same with the valiums."

I suggested we take her to a professional. "Let them take care of her," I said.

Nico shook his head, disgusted. "Let her die in her home," he said.

Nico spoke to Tuesday as she tried to cough up the pills. "Have faith," he whispered, "go to sleep." He laid Tuesday down on her side. He kissed her stomach until she stopped moving. Once she'd finally passed, Nico pressed his head to hers and wept.

"Where do you want her buried?"

"I don't want her buried," he said, "I want her here."

"Here?"

"Here."

Nico sat and smoked in the passenger seat, holding Tuesday, at first speaking only to give me directions to the taxidermist. He'd never looked so tired.

"What's strange," Nico said, "is digging a hole for someone you love. I was a child when we left my mother in a hole. I was a teenager when we did the same with my sister. It's normal, I know that, but that doesn't make it any less strange."

"It's not like you can take people to the taxidermist," I said.

"Why not?" Nico laughed. "When I die, take me to the taxidermist. Take me to the taxidermist and tell them to close my eyes and lay me down, on my back. Give me a room and lay me down next to Tuesday. Leave me with Tuesday, and lock the door."

"If that's what you want," I said. I drove slowly, with both hands. The few cars on the road sped past ours with ease. When we passed a raccoon that'd been flattened to the pavement, Nico brought Tuesday to his lips. Then he spoke of his mother.

"She was young," he said, "thirty-three. She got sick in the heart and was in the hospital for about a month before she died. She told jokes to make us laugh, mainly my brother and my sister and me. To make things easier, I guess. It was what it was. Someday your mother will start to die, and while she's dying, she'll tell jokes, too. At first you'll cry, then you'll laugh, and then you'll cry some more. Eventually you learn to do both at the same time. I remember her there, in the hospital, smoking. The doctors all smoked then, too. They said smoking would be good for her, that it would help her relax. Dying, smoking, telling jokes. That was my mother. She taught us well. When she was getting close to the end, a sister of hers brought a priest to pray over her. My mother thought that was funny. When the priest walked into her hospital room, she told him not to waste his time. *Poor priest*, she said, *pray for the living*."

"And your father?" I asked.

"He was working in his office when his heart attacked. He was always working. It was his choice, I guess. Your father and me flew back to Colombia as soon as we heard. Your grandfather was in a coma when we arrived and your father made it clear to the doctors that we didn't want them to prolong the inevitable. *No heroics*, he told them. We decided not to bury him. We let the doctors take from him whatever might be useful to the living. I was against it at first, but I gave in to your father's pragmatism. It was what your grandfather would've wanted, after all. What was left of him was cremated. We spread the ashes atop his favorite mountain. I cried the way I always do, with my head in my hands and my eyes on the ground. I looked up at your father. He was crying, too. Of course he was. But he was standing. He had his hands in his pockets. He wasn't looking at the ground."

I almost missed the exit. Nico had to point it out to me just as I was about to pass it. It was dark and we were almost there.

"What about your sister?" I asked.

"It was as if life were a question," he said, "and her answer was no."

Nico carried Tuesday into the taxidermist's and laid her down on the counter. The taxidermist asked Nico how he'd like her to remain. "Make her asleep," he said.

CLASS OF 2016

At the time of my graduation, I had little experience with ceremony. My baptism, for example, I don't recall. The only thing I remember about my first communion is the stale taste of sacrament. That, and trying to come up with something to say to the priest during my first confession. I told him that I didn't always brush my teeth. I was never confirmed. My father never let me anywhere near a wedding. This was the direct product of his regrets over his own marriage. In all fairness, he wasn't exactly an institutional person to begin with. Everybody that died in my family had done so before I'd been born. The only funeral I'd ever taken part in, if it can be called a funeral, was Tuesday's.

Today, stranded in Ramona's house, I watch the local vultures soar in circles above our street. Slowly, they come closer to the earth. Eventually they land. The truth is I like to think that my entire life has been a ceremony of some kind, but I didn't think that way then.

Everyone looked funny in their hats and small in their robes, myself included. We were outside of the auditorium, madly arranging ourselves in alphabetical order, when Ms. Monti showed up. She only said goodbye to her favorite students. She gave me a big hug. I asked her if she was going to stick around for the ceremony. "No," she said, "I'm going on a first date." We congratulated one another. I looked her up this morning for the first time in years. It turns out she's married and expecting her first child.

We were the class of 2016. The speeches were optimistic and forgettable. Over the course of two hours, we were told seven times that we could go on to change the world. One by one our names were called. One by one we shook hands with the principals. The band played. We turned our tassels. Some people cried. I managed to feel some nostalgia. I wished people luck. I posed for pictures, mostly with Nico and my parents. I even took one with the principal. My parents thanked him for allowing me to graduate, despite my grades. "It's my job," he said.

The principal went on to ask about Ana. She'd graduated seven years before, but he remembered her well. She'd been an impressive student. She'd gotten great grades and had been highly involved in several extracurricular organizations. She had almost been elected president, too, losing two consecutive elections by relatively small margins. According to Ana, she would have won had she not been Colombian. She was probably right.

"She's a lawyer," my father said. "In Tucson."

The principal got excited. "What kind of law?"

"Immigration," my mother said.

The principal lifted his eyebrows. "Very interesting."

Ana messaged me after the ceremony. She said she was sorry she couldn't come. I understood, but I wished she'd called.

My family held a small celebratory dinner at the local Brazilian deli. We had picanha, chicken wrapped with bacon, rice and beans, and guava juice. After we finished eating, my mother handed me an envelope. It was a gift from the three of them. Inside were two plane tickets to Colombia.

I hadn't been in years, when my sister and I had traveled with my mother to spend time with her side of the family. My father had refused to go. He hadn't exactly been invited, anyway. According to my grandmother, he was to blame for my mother's faraway life in the United States. According to my father, his mother-in-law was to blame for his failed marriage.

I didn't know what I'd done to deserve a gift. I thanked them. Nico explained that he was the one that would go with me, that together we would see what was left of his family. I asked my parents if they were sure it was a good idea for Nico and me to go on vacation together.

"It's not a vacation," Nico said. "It's a trip."

CARTAGENA

Nico sat passenger in the taxi we hailed at the Cartagena airport. The driver asked Nico where he was coming from, then asked how long it'd been since he'd left Colombia. "A lifetime," Nico said.

The two spoke of war and peace. The driver asked Nico if America was actually capable of electing Trump. Nico said yes. When their conversation paused, Nico made a point to turn to the backseat and tell me that taxi drivers knew more about politics than anyone else. The driver's laminated headshot was displayed on the back of his seat. A rosary swayed from his rearview mirror. Statuettes of Jesus and Mary shook on the dashboard. I grew carsick. I rolled the window down and watched the ocean crash into the walls of the old city.

The hotel was a large house with white clay walls and ceramic tiles that kept the ground cool. While Nico settled our reservation with the concierge, I sat on a stool in the corner and tried to regain my senses. I closed my eyes and made myself still. A girl no older than fourteen or fifteen woke me from my nausea and handed me a cup of lime water. I thanked her.

I showered and dressed. While Nico did the same, I watched television. There was news of a murder, the weather, followed by extended coverage of the previous night's big soccer match. Independiente Medellín, rival to Nico's beloved Atlético Nacional, had won the final.

Nico exited the bathroom as footage played of the previous night's celebrations. "A sad day for humanity," he said.

We walked alongside the laguna. Nico would point at something, a little bar or café or market, and say something about how he'd spent time there during his stint with the navy. I don't remember all of what he said then because of how hot it was. I told Nico that I needed a break, to stop and sit for a little while, that blisters were beginning to form on my soles. It had only been an hour or so. I sat down to remove my shoes and take my chances barefoot. Nico stopped me. "You'll burn holes in your feet," he said. He offered to swap his sandals for my shoes.

"No," I said, "I'll be fine." He would've helped me, I'm sure, but he seemed satisfied with me for declining his offer.

We stopped at a small lunch spot by the laguna, a square concrete shack surrounded by small tables bolted to the ground. Nico ordered a platter of fried mojarra, fried plantain, and coconut rice for us to share. I did most of the eating. Nico did most of the talking. I asked him why he'd joined the navy. "I didn't have a choice," he said, laughing. I nodded and kept eating. Nico took small, slow bites and drank from his beer to wash down his food. When he swallowed it looked like he was swallowing medicine.

"I was your age when I got drafted," Nico said. "Mandatory military service. Two years. Half of my friends got lucky and weren't picked to serve. Others had rich, well-connected parents who pulled some strings to get them out of it. My father didn't have the money or the clout. Even if he had, I'm not so sure he would've helped me. He thought it would be good for me to serve. It was, in a way. I suppose I learned some things. The navy taught me how to shower and shave in two minutes. How to make my bed. How to march. How to keep my mouth shut. What Cartagena taught me was even more important."

We finished the ceviche and took the last sips of our beers.

"Like what?" I asked.

Nico grinned. "Among other things, how to sing and how to dance."

We walked to the old part of town; the part carefully preserved and surrounded by tall stone walls built by the Spanish to protect themselves from the ocean, and whoever tried to cause them trouble. It was a fortress. It was a popular place to export gold and import slaves.

Our guide was a tall dark man with round glasses. He approached us at the entrance of the old city and asked us if we'd like a tour. After a quick negotiation, he was hired. He'd been born and raised in Cartagena and he'd never left. He taught literature and history at a public high school a few miles away from the airport. He told little jokes that were only half funny. I liked him. Nico called him Professor.

"Professor," Nico asked, "what are you going to teach us?"

"I'm going to say a lot," he said, "but what you need to remember is this. The Spaniards stole the land from the natives and built the city using the natives' buried riches. Then the city became the capital of slave trading in the Americas, and a key port for the exportation of silver and gold. For centuries, Europeans warred against one another over control of the land. Walls were built. Disease and starvation ravaged the city. Eventually, after more war, Colombia became independent from Spain. And here we are." Nico nodded along, pleased with the Professor's introduction. He turned to me and pinched my ear between his fingers, neither gently nor harshly.

We circled the old city for about an hour or so. In the streets, tourists bought paintings of traditional balconies overflowing with flowers from street vendors and posed for pictures with women selling fruit. They were amazed by the way the women balanced large woven baskets on the tops of their heads. Nico tapped me on the shoulder and gestured to the tourists dressed in safari gear with their cameras hanging from their sunburned necks. I laughed. The Professor laughed, too.

There were churches everywhere, some of them beautiful. "The Spanish had more money than they could count," the Professor said. "They didn't know where to put it, so they built churches one next to the other."

The Professor pointed out a statue of an African prisoner and a Spanish priest who, according to the plaque, baptized around three hundred thousand slaves.

"Just what they needed," Nico said.

The Professor nodded. "That's how the story goes," he said.

The Professor offered to make us a list of good restaurants and music venues. Proudly, Nico declined, citing the years he was stationed in Cartagena with the naval academy. Nico and I thanked him for the tour. Before the Professor could leave, Nico handed him some money and asked him for a favor. We smoked a cigarette and waited for the Professor to come back. He slipped a pair of joints into Nico's shirt pocket and was on his way.

Nico proposed beer. I accepted. We sat down at a café and watched the tourists pass us by.

"Are you tired?" he asked.

I shook my head.

"Good," Nico said, "There's something you should see."

We finished our beers and thanked the boy who'd brought them to us. We walked into a large white building with unpainted wooden balconies. "This," he said, "is the Palace of Inquisition." Nico bought one ticket and put it in my palm. "I'll wait for you outside."

I asked Nico why he wasn't going in.

"I've seen it once. I don't need to see it twice."

There were no tourists and no guards. Aside from the ticket man, I was alone. The first floor was home to the museum's instruments of torture. There was the corda, the thumbscrew, the rack, and the wheel. Nearly eight hundred Jews, slaves, and women accused of witchcraft were executed for heresy. These murders were carried out by the Holy Office of the Inquisition.

A year after my visit, in 2017, Pope Francis visited Colombia. In his honor, the torture devices were removed from the Palace of Inquisition, only to be displayed again following his stay.

Across the street from the museum, a bronze statue depicted Simón Bolívar and his horse. I was reading the pedestal's engravements when I heard Nico's voice. He shouted the words engraved before me, a quote from Bolívar. "The entirety of America awaits its liberty and salvation!" I turned to see Nico sitting cross legged on a bench with a bottle of rum and two plastic cups. Smiling, he grabbed my cup and filled it. "Cheers," he said.

We walked to the edge of the old city and set up on a bench by the stone wall, below an old turret. A different crowd had begun to take over the town. We watched long lines of shiny, overdressed people form and grow outside a cluster of night-clubs. Popular colors included white, black, silver, and gold.

We were halfway done with the bottle when Nico began telling me a story.

"I knew a man," Nico said, "a friend of my father's. He had a typical man's name. I don't remember it. It doesn't matter. Normal guy. He was an accountant or an insurance agent. He did pretty well. But he drank too much. He drank at home and he drank at work. He liked whiskey but switched to vodka so people wouldn't be able to smell it on him. Eventually, his friends and family convinced him to stop. They made sure he didn't go to the bar, made sure there was no liquor at home or at the office. Do you know what he ended up doing?"

"What?" I asked.

"He began to buy his wife perfume. Bottle after bottle. Maybe it was a way of saying sorry, or thank you. Sometimes he bought her jewelry. Mostly, though, it was perfume. Every week or so, he would bring home a handful of new, expensive bottles. French, Italian, whatever. Why do you think?"

"Because he was sorry," I said, "because he was grateful."

"That's what you'd think, right? That's what she thought. That's what everyone thought. But no, that wasn't it. He bought his wife so much perfume that she'd lost track of all the perfume he'd given her. Just imagine all that perfume."

"Who needs that much perfume?" I asked.

"He did," Nico said.

"Why?" I asked. "To forgive himself?"

"No, no. He was *drinking* the perfume. Think about it. He found a way. A man drinking his wife's perfume. I don't know what it means. I know it means something. I've told people this story and all they've said is that it's sad. But of course it's sad. It's beautiful, I think. I mean, who drinks perfume?"

"A man with a typical name," I said.

"Right," Nico said, smiling. "You're right."

We ended up at a bar near the hotel. It was an older, local crowd, and there was a live band playing. Nico and I sat at a table near the back of the bar and watched. He leaned over and screamed in my ear. "Vallenato. The music they're playing is called vallenato. Pay attention to this song. Pay attention to the words."

I did just that. I did whatever Nico asked of me. I ignored the happy dancing couples, the young and the old, the beautiful men and women who moved in ways I knew, even then, I'd never be able to. The singer wailed into the microphone. Something about a missing fortune. Something about an honored rat that stole.

I had to help Nico on the way back to the hotel to keep him from falling. Growing up, I'd helped my drunk father and drunk sister several times. I knew the drill. Nico and I passed by two men talking to two prostitutes. One of the men used his finger to inspect her teeth. From what I could hear, he was negotiating the price.

We were halfway to our hotel when I decided to hail a taxi. I hoped it would be our driver from earlier that day, but it wasn't. Still, the driver helped me drag Nico onto the backseat.

"Is he going to vomit?" the driver asked.

"He won't," I said. "I promise."

The same girl who'd gifted me lime water in the morning was alone in the lobby. She didn't smile. She said hello and nothing else. She took Nico by the ankles and helped me carry him up the stairs and into the bathroom of our hotel room. I pulled a bill from my pocket and held it out to her, as if I were paying a toll.

I smoked a cigarette while I waited for Nico to finish vomiting. Once the dry heaving began, I flushed the toilet. I grabbed him, turned him flat on his back, and wiped the vomit from his face. I shook him until his eyes opened. I told him it was okay, that he was going to be fine. Even then, I knew I was lying. Nico shook his head and tried to speak. "Stop," I told him. I put the back of my hand against his face and decided he was too hot. I moved him to the shower and propped him up against the back of the tub. I washed him with cold water, wrapped him in a towel, and dragged him to bed. I put him on his side and made sure he was still breathing. He was. I kissed his forehead. I picked the newspaper up from the nightstand and read while I prayed for his heart to slow. I checked the weather forecast for Cartagena. It was only going to get hotter. I checked the forecast for Medellín. Rain. Nico's breathing normalized. His heart kept ticking. I folded the newspaper and set it back down on the nightstand. It was then that I noticed the headline on the front page. I read it aloud. I knew Nico could hear me. I said, "Gold miners say output has peaked."

We began our resurrection in the makeshift cafeteria adjacent to the hotel lobby. I didn't think I'd be able to stomach anything aside from a cup or two of coffee. I tried to convince Nico that I didn't need to eat anything. Thankfully, he ignored me. We feasted on arepa de huevo, empanadas, chicharrón, chorizo, rice, and beans. Nico requested a second order of the chicharrón.

"How do you feel?" I asked.

"Incredible," Nico said.

Nico and I laid our towels down just close enough to the tide so that the water would reach our feet. Nico made a point to tell me that the ancient cure to each and every hangover was to look directly at the sun for seven seconds. Somehow, I believed him. I made it to five seconds before I couldn't look any longer. Nico laughed at me, apologized, then laughed some more. Before long, Nico began snoring. I kept watch of the beach around us. In the shallowest water, naked babies splashed and screamed. The school-aged children took themselves more seriously. A group of six kids competed among themselves to see who could build the most impressive temporary castle. Eventually, the group outgrew their little game and retired to the waves. The deeper water was littered with teenage romances, each couple seemingly attached by the mouth.

A boy asked me if I wanted to buy a flower. Nico mumbled in his sleep. The boy made a joke of it and claimed that he'd clearly heard Nico say yes. I chose the healthiest orchid and asked the boy his name.

"Salvador," he said.

I watched him as he continued selling flowers to the world. I pressed the orchid to my nose until I got dizzy, then placed it on Nico's sleeping stomach. I closed my eyes. I woke up to Nico looking down at me, mouthing an urgent question. "Who gave me this orchid?"

We swam, showered, and returned to the old city. After consulting a few locals, Nico was able to locate a favorite restaurant of his. Once there, we shared a large cauldron of fish soup and a pitcher of sugar cane water. Nico said that our day together had been one of the best hangovers he'd ever had. Of the very few hangovers I'd experienced before then, that one with Nico was easily the best. I told him so. He laughed. "That's not saying much," he joked, "but thank you."

Before easing into an early, responsible sleep, Nico and I positioned ourselves, once again, on the bench at the edge of the old city. I listened as Nico soberly lectured me about money. He spoke of silver. He spoke of gold. He spoke of entire peoples in the Americas who had decided to commit mass suicide before the Inquisition could wash upon their shore.

"We had the land," Nico said, "and now we have the Bible."

"We?" I asked.

I didn't know it then, but that night was the last time Nico stood before an ocean. We were walking along the shoreline, the water washing over the tops of our tired feet.

"The ocean," Nico said, "it isn't that beautiful."

MEDELLÍN

On our short flight to Medellín, Nico read the paper while I flipped through the in-flight magazine. He had shaved that morning and ironed his clothes, somehow managing to make himself look like someone who belonged in the front row of a plane. Halfway through the flight, Nico handed me the newspaper pages he'd already consumed. The major headline reported that a group of American soldiers had been arrested for attempting to smuggle a million dollars' worth of cocaine from Colombia to the United States aboard a military plane. "Such is life in the tropics," Nico said.

According to Nico, Medellín required a rental car. He claimed it was too dangerous to hail taxis on the street. The airport was in Rionegro, about an hour-long drive from the city. As we descended from the mountains into the valley, Nico lamented the housing developments and shopping malls that lined the highway.

"This used to be green," he said, "all green. Every other Sunday, your grandfather would drive us through the mountains, just to see them and smell them. Now this."

Nico had gone mostly quiet about half an hour into the drive. In that time, we drove circles around a city that Nico no longer recognized. When Nico did speak, he only did so in an effort to reassure me that he wasn't lost. At each intersection, I watched the flower vendors march through traffic.

With the help of a taxi driver at a red light, Nico was able to secure directions to our destination. Originally, I'd figured we would be staying in a hotel similar to the one we'd enjoyed in Cartagena. Instead, we pulled up to a small guardhouse outside of a gated community not too far from downtown. Nico exchanged pleasantries with the guard. A German shepherd stood attentively beside him. The guard asked Nico his name, then asked who he was visiting.

"Rocío," Nico said. The guard held a phone to his ear and kept his eyes on Nico. I asked Nico who Rocío was. "Violeta's mother," he said.

"Violeta?" I asked.

"My girlfriend," Nico said. "The one who died."

The shepherd followed our rental car a few hundred feet downhill. When I stepped out, the shepherd looked at me, sniffed my crotch, and then licked my hand. Nico laughed, then ordered me to unload our luggage from the backseat. Rocío's hunched, frail figure emerged from the front of her yellow home. The shepherd ran to her and burrowed its head between her knees. I was afraid the dog would knock her over, but Rocío smiled as she scratched the shepherd's ears. Nico and Rocío embraced. I watched as Rocío wiped a tear from her eye with her shaking hand.

"How long," she said.

"Too long," Nico said.

Nico referred to her as Doctor. "Doctor," he said, "this is Gregorio."

"A pleasure to meet you," I said. Rocío gripped my hand with both of hers and demanded that I make myself at home.

I asked if the shepherd was hers. "No," she said, "he belongs to everyone."

The three of us sat smoking on the back patio, overlooking a small patch of forest that stood between Rocío's gated community and a set of high-rise apartments. Rocío pointed out that, if one listened closely enough, one could hear the water running through the creek behind the trees. I did my best to listen, but only managed to hear the traffic.

"Can you hear it?" Rocío asked.

"Yes," I said, lying.

I listened as Rocío and Nico caught up on one another's lives. Rocío talked about her retirement from the hospital and her position as chair of the university's medical department. She still attended meetings every now and then to ensure, in her words, that the hospital maintained its decency. At one point, Nico let out an ugly cough. Rocío watched him. "I don't like the sound of that," she said.

"Neither do I," laughed Nico.

I did what I was told and made myself at home by lying in a hammock on the patio. Rocío insisted on providing me with a proper bed for a proper nap. She led me to a small room at the end of a long dark hallway on the first floor. I took position in the small twin bed and let my feet hang over the end of the mattress. On one nightstand, there was a picture of a young woman with shoulder length hair in a cap and gown. On the other nightstand, there was a picture of a young Nico and the same young woman. Violeta. They were both dressed well, he in an oversized suit, and she in a long loose dress. Her face was turned toward his and tilted back in laughter. Nico's eyes were open slightly as he yawned into the camera. I, too, yawned. I did what I could to settle into the empty room. I closed my eyes and fell into an odd, light sleep from which I could hear Rocío's and Nico's voices as clearly as if I were awake. I tried to move and couldn't. I tried to call out to them, but my mouth wouldn't open.

"Not much time," I heard Rocío say.

"Not much time at all," Nico said. After a short silence, they laughed. Nico's laugh turned into another heavy cough. "This cancer's going to kill me," he said.

Calmly, Rocío told Nico of something that happened to her only months before, in December.

"Nico," she said, "there were four or five of them. All armed, all masked. They woke me up, undressed me, and tied me to the chair. This is no world to live in. They threatened me for hours. One of them, the youngest of the group, was nice enough to feed me cigarettes while the others sorted through the house. They looked everywhere."

"What did they take?" Nico asked.

"Not much," Rocío said. "Some jewelry and some art. In the end, the sun came up and our shepherd barked and the four of them left before the guard could catch them, as if he could've done anything if he had. And that was that. A week later, I sat around a linen table and led what's still left of my family in a prayer I couldn't have believed less in. And I said nothing about what happened, and I ate my dinner, and I laughed when jokes were told, and I smiled at the camera each and every time it was pointed at me."

I woke up in a sweat and returned to the patio as if I had slept well and overheard nothing. "I want to show you something," Rocío said. She pointed to a basket beneath the fireplace. Inside were scraps of burned metal. I set the basket down on the coffee table between the three of us. I looked at Nico and he nodded as if to say, *Listen*. Rocío removed a piece of metal from the basket and held it up to me.

"I assume you know something about this country," she said.

"Yes," I said. "Something."

She explained to me, with the metal in her hand, that the pieces were from a car that had been bombed a few blocks from her home. "This home," she said. A tear fell from her eyes and the rest of her face didn't move.

"These pieces," she said, "they rained on us. They rained on our roof and they rained on our lawn. The impact from the bomb took the front door down. We had to rebuild part of the house. I don't know why I kept the pieces. Actually, I do know why. I didn't know how to throw them away."

I fished a piece of metal from the pile and held it with both hands. One of its edges caught the side of my left thumb. It was a small cut but the blood came quickly.

The plan for the evening, it turned out, was for Nico and I to watch a bullfight. "Why?" I asked.

"Tradition," Nico said, shrugging. "It's something you should see at least once."

Rocío explained. "They won't be around much longer. They're being outlawed around the world, around the country."

"There are only so many bullfights left," Nico said.

"Good," I said.

Nico promised Rocío we'd be back for dinner. "Are you sure you know where you're going?" she asked.

We drove into the city. Nico pointed out a small square building on one of the busiest streets. It stood out, somehow, despite being surrounded by office buildings and malls and hotels and casinos. "I grew up in that house," Nico said. "Now it's a bank."

Together we sat through the mid-afternoon traffic. The sky grayed and the rain came slowly. Nico rolled the windows up and continued smoking. I joined him. At every red light, children and adults marched through the traffic, selling flowers, phone chargers, and umbrellas in the drizzling rain.

We parked in a gravel lot a few blocks away from the bullring, where the three teenagers on duty played cards in the guardhouse. A sign on the window listed the parking rates and the name of the venue nearby: Plaza de Toros La Macarena. Nico asked the teenagers if the rain was strong enough for the bullfight to be canceled. "No, no," one of the teenagers said, "only if it pours."

As we entered the bullring, I overheard an older couple talking about a car bombing that had taken place at La Macarena some twenty-five years before, ordered by Pablo Escobar. I asked Nico if it was true. "Of course it's true. One bombing of many."

From the highest bleacher, Nico and I could see the entirety of the ring: the bull, the band, the president, the matador, and most importantly, the audience. As we sipped on our first beers, the band began to play the matador into the ring. Nico elbowed me. "Bulls are color blind," he said. "The cape is red to hide the blood."

"Who are you rooting for?" I asked.

"The bull. Every time."

I had grown up believing that bullfights took place between one man and one bull. Why, I don't exactly know. I imagine my misconception had to do with being, from birth, consistently bombarded by the many mythologies of a man, alone, capable of achieving something great, or more to the general point, defeating something, or someone, categorically evil. The truth, I learned, is that a bullfighter is never alone. I watched as the bullfighter began the fight with two horsemen and ended with two matadors.

The fight must've lasted an hour, or more. I don't know who was most at fault. Maybe the lancers didn't lance properly. Perhaps the matador missed the mark with his two small flags. It's possible that the bull was extraordinary, though no one, Nico included, made any comments about the bull's pedigree.

Everything indicated that we were in the presence of a mediocre sacrifice. When it came to the third and last part of the bull-fight, the matador repeatedly failed to execute the bull. "He's supposed to kill the bull quickly," Nico said. The crowd jeered louder and louder with each stab. The bull bled all over and struggled to run. A trumpet warned the matador to hurry up and finish the job. He continued to disappoint. The trumpeter blew again, then again, and finally the fight was over. The bull, it seemed, had won.

"A happy ending," I said.

Nico shook his head. "They kill the bull anyway."

We left the bullring a different way than we'd entered. "Where are we going?" I asked.

"I want you to see something," Nico said.

Nico walked quickly. He didn't look at me to see if I was keeping up. He didn't seem to be looking at anything. His head didn't turn and his stride didn't change. We crossed a busy street and reached an open plaza, Parque San Antonio.

He stopped next to what looked like two large, round sculptures. Two fat birds cast in bronze. Once there, I understood that they were not only two birds, but twin doves.

Nico stood in front of the eldest dove. I walked around it. From behind I could see him through its exploded middle. I wiped my eyes and moved closer to the dove. I saw Nico's mouth moving but did not hear him. I imagined a version of Nico's life void of war. A life with Violeta and their children. A world in which he could have stayed.

I stood parallel to Nico, in front of the unharmed dove. Water ran down its face, its chest, and off its grounded claws. I felt something move behind me, then a hard something pressed onto the side of my stomach. A voice spoke softly into my ear.

"Do not move," it commanded, "do not speak." I felt my phone leave my pocket. Then my wallet. I turned to Nico. His eyes were still fixed on the open dove.

"Nico," I said, "they robbed me, they robbed me."

Nico didn't speak until we were halfway to Rocío's. His words came out slow and labored. "I'll buy you a new phone," he said. "And I'll give you however much money you had."

"Nico, it wasn't your fault."

"It doesn't matter," he said.

Rocío prepared arroz flojo, a traditional Antioquian dinner that had become a rarity. She joked that she was the only person left in Medellín who still knew how to make it. The dish consisted of white rice soup, powdered beef, fried eggs, home fried potatoes, morcilla, and avocado. As she loaded her bowl with meat, she explained that her doctor had ordered her to eat more iron. "When people ask me how I'm doing," she said, "I tell them that I'm perfect from the neck up."

Nico laughed, then jumped in with a joke of his own. "When people ask me how I'm doing, I tell them I'm doing bad."

"Just like that?" Rocío asked.

"Like that. One word. *Bad*. But they rarely ask."

Over dinner, Rocío caught Nico up on the lives, deaths, successes, and failures of people they had in common. It turned out that one of their mutual friends, a childhood classmate of Nico's, was a key player in the Colombian peace process being brokered between the government and the FARC. "The longest ongoing civil war in the world," Rocío said.

Nico nodded. He took a deep breath. "Wars don't end."

"This one could, finally," answered Rocío, her hands held open over the table, as if asking Nico to comply.

"I don't see it," he said. "Two hundred thousand dead. Seven million displaced. And what about the False Positives?" Nico turned to me. "The military murdered thousands of innocent people. Entire towns of people. And you know what they did after they killed them? They framed the dead as guerilla combatants. Publicized the killings in the media as victories over the enemy. Totally innocent people killed by the thousands. Five or six thousand, probably more. All for a little propaganda. All to win a war. *Peace?* What peace?"

"Everything your uncle is saying is true," Rocío said. "All I'm saying is that progress is possible. Peace, maybe not. But progress, yes, it is possible. Things can be better. Improvement is achievable and optimism is important."

"You're right, Rocío. You're right." Nico pulled a cigarette from his pocket. His hands shook as he started it. "All I know is this. I was born after this war started, and I will be dead before it ends."

We were out on the porch, the three of us, smoking our last cigarette of the night. The shepherd slept at our feet. "So," Rocío said, "how are the doves?"

ENVIGADO

The next afternoon, Nico took me to Envigado to eat morcilla and empanadas. The morcilla was the best I've ever had. The empanadas were greasy, but good. The truth is I prefer Argentinian empanadas to Colombian empanadas. I said so to Nico. "Sometimes," he said. We continued eating. He took a sip from his beer as he looked out onto the plaza, where a small group of children were playing a game of soccer. A group of American tourists were being led across the square, through the soccer game, by an animated tour guide. One of the children pretended to kick the ball at one of the tourists, causing him to flinch and drop his phone. He and his partner screamed at the children. The children laughed.

Another member of the tour group was wearing a t-shirt with a mugshot of a young Pablo Escobar printed on the front. "Narco-Tourism," Nico said bitterly. He explained that Medellín was becoming a trendy city to visit for foreigners who idolize Escobar. "They're probably going to La Catedral," Nico said.

"La Catedral?" I asked.

"The prison Pablo Escobar designed for himself. He was facing extradition to the United States, his biggest fear, so he agreed to go to prison here in Colombia. The caveat was that he would customize the prison as he saw fit. He built a mansion on the mountain, here in Envigado, the town where he'd grown up, and stayed there for a couple of years. He lived like a free man. He hired his friends and associates as guards and continued to run his empire." Nico laughed as he finished his beer. "Today, it's a Benedictine monastery."

For hours, we sat, drank, and smoked in the plaza. Mostly, Nico talked about Pablo Escobar. The thousands of people he'd murdered, the generations he'd terrorized. The thousands of poor people he'd helped. Envigado, for example, was the first town in Colombia to have universal health care. "He's the most famous Colombian there's ever been," Nico said. "For most people around the world, Pablo Escobar is the only idea that exists of this country. Pablo, cocaine, and coffee."

"And flowers," I said.

Nico shook his head. "No, not flowers. Not even that."

We ended up drinking red wine at an Argentinean bar around the corner. We ordered a plate of empanadas, then another. "It's a tie," he concluded with a smile. A guitarist played tango after tango in the corner of the empty dancefloor. Nico spoke into my ear. "My father had a saying. I don't know where he got it from. For all I know, he might've come up with it himself. The saying changed depending on how much he'd had to drink." Nico got distracted and began singing along with the song. He was drunk.

"What was the saying?" I asked.

Nico began to cry. "Life is a tango and whoever dances is an asshole."

I put my hand on Nico's shoulder. He looked me in the eyes and nodded.

"What was the other version?" I asked.

"Life is a tango," Nico said, "and whoever *doesn't* dance is an asshole."

"Which one do you like better?" I asked.

"I love both," Nico said.

BOGOTÁ

We left Medellín early the next morning. Before driving to the airport, we enjoyed a box of pastries Rocío had brought especially for Nico from one of the oldest bakeries in the city. Their buñuelos and pandebonos had been his favorite treats growing up. Rocío and I enjoyed a couple of each. Nico devoured the rest, savoring each bite. I remember him speaking with a mouthful of bread. Like a child. "Thank you, Rocío. Thank you."

When Rocío and Nico said goodbye, they said they'd see each other soon.

Nico was never the same again. He was, I believe, happy. Or relieved. Or ready, finally, to die. He was tired. Very tired, but at peace. He fell asleep before the plane took off in Medellín and woke up when we landed in Bogotá. When he opened his eyes, it was as if he was surprised that he'd returned to earth. He looked at me and smiled. "I'm still here," he said.

We were pulling our luggage along the jet bridge to the terminal. Nico's hair was a mess. He looked at the ground before him as he talked. "I dreamed of my family," Nico said. "My mother and my father and my sister. Tuesday and Violeta."

"What did they say?"

"That they were waiting for me."

We would only be in Bogotá for the day. Our flight back to the United States left at midnight. The tickets were cheaper and would take us directly to New York.

"What do you want to do before we go?" Nico asked, warmly.

"Whatever you want," I said.

"A museum?" Nico asked.

"Perfect," I said.

The Museum of Gold was created in the 1930s to preserve the cultural identity of the country. Most of the museum's artifacts were created prior to the Spanish conquest. It's home to fifty-five thousand pieces in total, most of them pure gold. They once belonged to nine different cultures: Calima, Muisca, Quimbaya, San Agustín, Tairona, Tierradentro, Tolima, Urabá, and Zenú. The museum is owned and operated by Colombia's national bank. Nico laughed when he told me this. He was also shaking his head.

For hours, I followed Nico through the dimly lit museum. He studied every piece with his face inches from the glass and his hands clasped behind his back. I have a perfectly clear memory of one artifact, made by the Muisca, which depicts a ritual offering on Lake Guatavita. The zipa, covered in gold dust, would lead his soldiers out to the middle of the sacred lake. There, they would toss their offerings to the gods into the water. Emerald, silver, and gold. Finally, the zipa would abandon the raft and swim.

I remember Nico glowing before the raft, his long face bathed in gold. When I think of Nico, that is the Nico I love to remember most. He looked at me with golden eyes, with golden teeth. "Look, Gregorio. Look."

ENDS OF GAMES

Colombia had been the pre-tournament favorite for the 1994 FIFA World Cup. They had played beautifully throughout the qualification stage, defeating the Argentinian national team in Buenos Aires by a score of 5-0. Argentina were the defending Copa América champions and had not lost a game on their home soil in over six years. After the final whistle, the stadium, including Diego Maradona, gave the Colombian team a standing ovation.

Colombia was eliminated in the first round after placing last in a group of four teams. That group included the United States, the World Cup's host country. They faced one another at the Rose Bowl, in Los Angeles. The United States won the match by one. Andrés Escobar, Colombia's best defender, scored an own goal. Ten days later he died in Medellín. He was shot six times. According to witnesses, the killer shouted *gol* each time he pulled the trigger.

Growing up, I heard this story every time the national team played, any time an own goal was scored, or simply whenever Nico, my father, or my mother felt like reminiscing about that Colombian team, what could've been and wasn't. They had watched hundreds of matches together, the Andrés Escobar game included. It was a tradition that began when Nico and my father were young boys. Every other Sunday they would go to the stadium with their parents and sister. When they didn't go to the stadium, they watched at home, crowded around the living room television. The tradition continued after my parents married. It was something the three of them enjoyed doing together, almost weekly. The tradition eventually included my sister and me. It was like church.

After Nico and I returned from Colombia, we gathered in Nico's home to watch the 2016 Copa América Final on a warm Sunday night in June. Sadly, Colombia had lost the semi-final to Chile, the defending champions. The final featured the same teams as the previous Copa América. Argentina versus Chile. The game was set to take place in New Jersey. Had Nico's health been better, and had Colombia made the final, we might have made the long drive to attend. Instead, the four of us, my mother, father, Nico, and I, decided to share a dinner at home as we watched.

That Sunday morning, my mother called Nico and asked him what he'd most like to eat. I heard him tell my mother that whatever she wanted, or whatever was easiest, was more than fine. I heard her insist through the phone. Nico laughed, then answered honestly. "Arepas would be great," he said. "Some white cheese, some avocado, some eggs."

My mother asked what he'd like to drink.

Nico smiled. "Orange juice," he said. "Fresh orange juice."

My parents arrived an hour before the game, around seven. My father carried frozen arepas in one hand and a fifth of rum in the other. My mother held a bag of fresh oranges, a juicer, and a grocery bag with every other ingredient Nico had requested.

They told Nico not to stand and instead hugged him where he sat, on the couch in front of the television. My mother kissed Nico warmly. My father hugged him carefully, so as not to hurt him. My parents and I stood awkwardly in the living room as the pre-game show played in the background. Nico broke the silence. He tried and failed to contain a laugh. "Okay," he said, "everyone get to work."

The game itself wasn't memorable. Neither team played well. There was a lot of complaining, gamesmanship, and time wasting. One player from each team received a red card. The match ended scoreless, despite two periods of extra time. All in all, it was a blur. What I remember clearly was how the four of us sat in the living room, my mother on the couch with Nico, my father in a chair by the window, smoking, and I cross-legged on the carpet. The arepas were excellent. The orange juice was even better. My father poured rum into his and offered to pour some into everyone else's cups as well. Nico and my mother declined. My mother rarely, if ever, drank. Nico didn't feel well. I accepted.

The final, it turned out, would be decided by penalties. While we waited for them to begin, we talked about the cruelty of it all. How one or two players' misses would follow them for the rest of their lives. In many cases, even great players were best remembered for their mistakes. Even still, field players are remembered far more often than the goalkeepers. Not one of us mentioned them at all. I think back on that conversation as I lie on Ramona's couch, the curtains drawn to keep the light out. My head weighs more than the rest of me. Goalkeepers are, at best, secondary to the plot. They are supposed to fail. Failure is their job.

"The best players always miss," Nico said.

"Is that true?" I asked.

"Not always," my father said, "bad players miss, too. But it's true that great players miss often. Baggio, the best player in the world at the time, cost Italy the World Cup Final in 1994. He sent his penalty kick to the moon."

"I remember that one," my mother said. "Brazil won."

"Platini and Zico in 1986," Nico said.

My father answered. "John Terry in 2008. Team captain. If he'd made it, they would've won the Champions League. He slipped and sent his shot wide."

"Speaking of Champions League. Riquelme in 2006," Nico said, "Messi and Robben in 2012."

"Who was it that missed three in one game?" my mother asked.

Nico and my father laughed. They answered at the same time. "Martín Palermo."

I asked Nico and my father if they'd ever taken penalties before. If they'd missed. I didn't ask my mother because she never played soccer or any other sport. Her lowest grade in high school was physical education, her only bad one.

My father was the first to answer. He put out his cigarette as he began speaking. "I took two. I remember them like they happened yesterday. One was in a high school tournament, the other in university. I missed in high school. I sent it over the crossbar. Way over. We lost because of me. I wanted the ground to eat me. I had nightmares about it, here and there, for years. I dreamed of that miss until I scored the penalty in university." He took a long sip from his drink. He laughed. "I didn't feel happiness. What I felt was relief."

"I remember that game," Nico said.

"Which one?" my father asked.

"When you missed," Nico said. "I was there. You cried on the bus ride home. A tear or two, no more than three, but I noticed."

"It's true," my father said. "Do you remember what you said to me?"

"No," Nico said.

"You said, *I would've missed too.*"

My father lit another cigarette. My mother leaned over, asking him for a drag. "Nico," she said, "did you ever take a penalty?"

Nico shook his head.

"Why not?" I asked.

"I was too scared."

Chile's best player, Arturo Vidal, missed the first penalty of the shootout. Argentina's Lionel Messi, the best player in the world, missed the second. According to my father, he was the best player he'd ever seen. Nico preferred Diego Maradona.

Messi was on the verge of tears throughout the rest of the penalties. Everyone else was able to convert, except for another Argentinian player, Biglia, who had his penalty saved by Claudio Bravo. When this save was made Messi began to cry, despite the game not being over. When they finally lost, he began to sob. Openly. Coaches consoled him. Teammates consoled him. The Chilean players did so as well. He continued sobbing. We were mostly quiet as we watched. Several times my mom muttered the same phrase she always did during shootouts. "Penalties are not fair."

All the focus falls on the players who fail to score. It's as if the goalkeeper doesn't exist. The cruelest part, I believe, is that even when a goalkeeper makes a save, it's the shooter who has missed.

Messi retired from the national team after that match. He said he'd tried everything. They'd reached four major finals in a row and lost each one.

I helped my mother tidy up the kitchen as the night approached its ending. My father was in his chair by the window, smoking and looking at his phone. The post-game show murmured on the television.

Suddenly, Nico spoke loudly. "Mom," he said. He pointed to the corner of the living room.

I looked at my father, who looked at my mother, who was looking at me. "Nico," I said. I was going to tell him he was imagining things when my mother put a finger to her lips. She shook her head.

Nico gestured to my father. "Look. It's our mom."

My father looked to the corner and nodded. "What is she saying?"

"She's asking if we need anything."

"What do you need?" my father asked.

"Milk," Nico said. "Warm milk."

My mother filled a glass with milk and placed it in the microwave. She pulled it out before the machine could beep and added a straw. She brought it to Nico. He looked up at her and held out his arms.

Nothing else got said. We watched Nico as he drank the milk. He held the glass the way a child holds their bottle. Something in him changed, late that night, for the better. He was relieved.

My parents both gave Nico warm, loving goodbyes. My mother was fighting back tears. My father, too. They kissed his face and his head. My father pressed Nico to his chest. From where I stood, I could see Nico's hands squeezing my father's back, making a fist with his shirt.

Their car's headlights stayed on in the driveway for some time. Ten, maybe twenty minutes passed before I went to check on them, before I went to see if everything was okay. Through the windshield I saw them. My mother crying in the driver's seat. My father sobbing in her lap.

NICO DIES

Nico lasted most of the summer. When things were good, the time passed quickly. We watched game shows, talk shows, and soccer. We did crosswords. We barbecued with my parents and sat on the lawn. We built fires. We made candles. We drank coffee and we drank rum.

One night, I asked Nico if he would have done anything differently with his life.

Nico thought about the question for a good minute until a grin spread across his face. He nodded. "Yes. I would've worked harder. Rigorously. Every day."

I'd never laughed so hard. Nico laughed softly, as hard as he could.

Toward the end, what Nico did most was sleep. He was more asleep than awake. This was for the best. When he could no longer walk, I would carry what was left of him to the bathroom. Every few days I would bathe him, in bed. When I did, he would pretend to sleep. Soon after he stopped eating. He could barely breathe. I remember wetting his lips at our Sunday lunch so they would stop bleeding. My parents couldn't help but weep. Nico tried to speak. Once he gave up trying, he closed his eyes and turned his head.

A week before he died, Nico had asked me to promise him I wouldn't hold a formal funeral. When I'd asked him if he'd like to be taken to the taxidermist, he laughed and said he'd changed his mind. "Dig me a hole and plant me an orchid."

I watched Nico's ribs rise and fall with each breath. "Do you want to take anything with you?" I asked.

"Tuesday," Nico said.

"And what about the rest?"

Nico smiled. "All proceeds go to the living."

It happened in August, on a Saturday. I had gone out to get groceries for Sunday lunch. I came back with a few pounds of lamb, some vegetables, and limes for rum. When I came home, Nico had stopped breathing. Nico, finally, had gone home.

I called my parents and told them I'd found Nico dead in his sleep. While I waited for them to arrive, I read the letter Nico left me.

NICO'S LETTER

Gregorio:

We were both born in the fall. I in the rainy October of Medellín; you in the North American November, the month when the leaves turn and die, only to be raked into piles and burned. Fall is not my favorite season. For me, it is second to spring.

As an infant you seldom cried. You were born, it seemed, remarkably civil. As a child you rarely spoke. With each passing year your parents grew more concerned. They asked themselves what would happen to you if you didn't learn to speak freely. The answer, we concluded, was nothing. We agreed there were worse outcomes for a person. Much, much worse.

I was, I've been told, no different as a child. Like you, I spoke very little. When prompted by my parents, my brother and sister, I answered with as few words as possible. I was like many children, afflicted with a nervousness that would only begin to subside years later with the help of some substance—in my case, sweet liquor and all the cigarettes I could smoke. What I did not realize until I was much older was that my nerves had less to do with my fear of being noticed, and more to do with my disdain for the relentless protagonism of others.

I'm writing to you from the kitchen table. You are asleep in your room, on your back, with your hands clenched at your sides. The expression on your face is one of distress. In a few hours you will wake up and head straight to the kitchen sink, where you will chug a pint of water from the faucet. When I ask you how you've slept, you will say you slept well. Perhaps you are the type who lives harsh dreams and forgets all about them upon waking. It's possible you don't remember your dreams at all. Lately, I've slept very little. When I manage to sleep, it is brief. Each time I wake up I am more tired than before. I wake up on my side, with my knees tucked into my chest and my head curled inward. I haven't slept this way since I was young.

The crickets sang loud late into the night. The birds sang early. All summer they sing. All my life they sang. These days, I believe they're singing for me.

This is the last letter I will ever write; the fourth I've written this week. The first was for your beloved mother. For her I recalled some of our better memories: the births of you and your sister, the many Christmases, the occasional trips to the city and the coast. I thanked her for all the ways in which she loved me—as a sister, as a friend. She's the first person we all went to with news, be it great or terrible. Her marriage to your father is over, sure, but I insist that it wasn't a failure. They got very far, together. If there's anything I want for your mother now, it's for her to live her life and worry about herself. *Choose to choose*, I wrote. For now, she is choosing to return to Colombia, to her mother and sister, to the many debts she feels she owes. How lucky they are to have her. How lucky we were, too.

I can't say I offered your father any advice, really. The only decision I may have asked your father to make was to get a dog or two. He always preferred dogs. As children, we enjoyed the company of seven. Your father took more care of them than any of us. He fed them. Played with them. Bathed them. I wrote to your father, *Your next life should look a little like your first.* The truth is your father will soon be the only one of my family left alive. He will be alone with all our family's memories, and all our ghosts. Who better to share that solitude with than a good dog that never leaves?

I was very honest with your sister, more honest with her than ever. She has always been especially good at not hearing things she didn't want to hear. Just as I was incredible at keeping my thoughts to myself. I could have helped her. I could have helped her more, I should say. What I wrote to her was relatively simple. Like her, I was the first to leave home. Also like her, I enjoy my drinks. In my letter to her, I summarized the matter as easily as I could. I wrote: *The less you drink, the more control you'll have over your life.* I communicated one more thing, a message I believe to be far more important than the others. I demanded she understand that she is not alone in the world.

This I've said before, Gregorio. There is only one kind of letter, a love letter. To really write one, you must be sorry. In each of these four letters I'm sorry for the same reason. I'm sorry I couldn't tell you all what I've written sooner. I'm sorry I didn't speak when I should have. I didn't know how.

This last letter is at once the easiest and the hardest to write. For weeks I've asked myself what it is I want to tell you that I haven't already. For three months you've been more than a nephew, more than a friend. Gregorio, I owe you more than I have to give.

The truth is there is at least one thing I have given you. Your name. The day you were born, your parents were having a difficult time choosing. I recalled the dog your father had loved most as a child. A large, loving mutt named Gregorio. He had a rough burlap coat, round brown eyes, and large ears that moved with each neighborhood sound, no matter how distant. Your father adored that dog. Often, Gregorio would wander off and return a day or two later. One night he came home bleeding. I remember your father tending to him. How he cleaned and bandaged the large wound with rubbing alcohol and a healthy padding of gauze, then bathed him with a wet towel. Unlike many dogs, Gregorio calmly trusted your father with the makeshift surgery. He simply lay on the cool tile of the kitchen floor, crying softly. When your father was finished, Gregorio licked your father's hands gratefully. He leaned his large head into your father's chest and closed his eyes to rest.

Your grandmother gave Gregorio, the dog, his name. He was a quiet puppy, and, in a strange way, human. The etymology didn't, as it rarely does, lie. Gregorio—alert and watchful.

I realized there in the hospital room with your father and mother, your young sister and your newborn self, that the name held true for you as well. You were in your father's arms, wide-eyed and calm. Quiet. "Gregorio," I said. Your eyes opened wider even. Your head turned the slightest bit. Your large ears, I swear to God, they moved.

For some time you've known that my days were numbered. I received the news from the doctor in late November, in the same hospital that you were born. Cancer. All over. Sometime over the course of the decade or so I'd neglected the doctor, a cancer had grown and spread throughout my body. Treatment could have bought me another year, maybe two. But I decided against it. The last place I wanted to be at the end of my life was in a hospital. I was given an estimate of six months. I decided to go home.

I told your father the news this past Christmas. I told him I wanted to keep my situation private, that it was between me and him. He asked me why. I told him I didn't want anything to change. He insisted on letting the family know. I'm glad he did. He said it was important for you to know death. He said it was the most important thing you could learn. He was right.

I had had the foolish plan to wither away, for the most part, alone. I grew weaker by the month. One afternoon, your father stopped by for a cup of coffee and saw that I was struggling. He insisted you come stay with me. He said we would take good care of each other. *I don't have much to offer him*, I said. Your father laughed at me, warmly. *Nico*, he said, *you don't have to give him anything. Just tell him what you wish you had known.*

My nephew, my friend—for months I have thought about what your father asked of me before we began to share this home. One thing I know, one thing I wish everyone understood, is this. I could have been born anybody. This is true of everyone. Every person, every being that has ever found itself on this planet.

Let me try to explain.

Perhaps I was the Muisca, a thousand years before Christ. Perhaps I mined salt in what is now Bogotá. I may have carried a golden knife. If I could choose, I would like to have been the one who built the raft, made of gold. Before our gold was mined. I know I was no king. If I was born to do anything, it was to build something worthy of being stolen. If I had been with the Muisca, and if I had been lucky, I would have stood ashore and watched a king cover himself in dusted gold, and I would have tossed what precious metal and stone I owned into the water where he swam.

I could have been the Spanish, searching and slaughtering my way to gold. Maybe I was Columbus and the natives discovered me lost at sea. It is possible, too, that I died sick and poor and ashamed of all the blood I had spilled. Of course, it is unlikely I was Columbus, or any of the other soldiers, priests, or poets who followed him across the ocean. It is more likely that I was one of the many horses who never loved them.

And who am I to say that I was a person before I was Nico? Who am I to say I was not the land? Who am I to say I was not the River Magdalena herself?

Gregorio—my friend, my nephew—we have been born into a world of war. Remember this, always. There is blood in our oil. There is blood in our batteries. There is blood in our sugar. The world we live in is made of this blood. Death is nothing short of law on this stolen land.

But let me be clear. You couldn't save this world if you tried. Do what you do best. Look and listen.

Do not obsess yourself with the spectacular. Know this. The pyramid is a tombstone. The opera is a circus. The pageant is a bullfight.

Concern yourself instead with the sacred. Find someone to love, make a home, and hope that they do not die. And, if you can, find God.

Just the other morning, you mentioned that you would like to work in a museum, as I had. I was touched, of course, but not surprised. A museum would suit you. You even posed the hypothetical of moving to Washington, D.C. A strange city, surely, riddled with its own spectacles. *It's the most powerful city in the world*, I said. *Yes*, you answered bluntly, *that's why I want to go.*

I've thought about that conversation for days. You were born, I've come to find, to be a witness in this world.

A sacred calling, no doubt. I think this little adventure will prove worthwhile. As will all your others, one way or another. Maybe you'll stay. Maybe you'll go elsewhere. Maybe you'll come back.

I'll leave you with one last piece of advice before you go. Be lucky. It's the best thing you can be in this life.

Gregorio, my nephew, my friend—do not cry for me. Life goes on. It always does.

Despite everything, my illness and all, these have been good months. Some of the best of my life, unquestionably, though I believe the best are yet to come. If it's up to me, I have no doubt what I'll choose. I want to live again. The same life but better.

Be good, Gregorio. Be lucky.

THE ASKING PRICE

After my parents dealt with the logistics of Nico's death, we buried Nico's ashes in his backyard. I dug the hole. I made sure to include Tuesday, cologne, coffee, rum, and a carton of cigarettes. My father included a blank check. "Just in case," he said. My mother added buñuelos and pandebonos. I planted the orchid. We cried for a while. Then we ate. We prepared lamb and we drank wine. All this in Nico's kitchen. My parents were making plans, predicting the future. When the house sold, my father would move into Nico's. I was welcome to stay. My mother would move to Santa Marta to take care of my grandmother. I was welcome to go. Generous as their offers were, I wasn't sold on either. Even if I'd had a preference, it would've been wrong to choose. I declined both. Ana remained in Tucson. Had she invited me to stay with her, I might have gone.

In the meantime, I moved back in with my parents. A week or so later their divorce was made official. It couldn't have gone better. There were no lawyers. There was nothing but agreement. My parents split everything in half. I went with them to court. The judge congratulated them and I did too. During the proceeding,

I thought back to the night my mother first threatened my father with a divorce. She'd already hired a lawyer. I was seven and my sister was fourteen. My parents were screaming at each other in the kitchen. Ana took me outside and sat with me on the front porch. She held me for hours. She put her hands over my ears. I wished my sister had been there in court with us. To celebrate.

Late that night, after trying to sleep and failing, I called her. She was drunk when she answered the phone. She sounded like another person.

"Who is this?" Ana slurred.

"It's me," I said.

"Who?"

"Gregorio," I said.

I heard shuffling in the background, a static through the phone. I pictured her lying on her couch, trying to sit up. She let out a long sigh. A glass chimed. A minute passed.

"Ana," I said. I repeated her name until she answered.

"What happened?" she asked.

"Mom and Dad divorced."

"It's about time," she said. Then she hung up.

The asking price was met and the house was sold. We had to be out by September. I had less than a month before I had to have an answer to the question of what was next for me. My only marketable skill was circumstantial. I grew up speaking Spanish. My parents gave me the idea to look for a job as a translator or interpreter. I wasn't opposed to the idea. It was license for me to go pretty much anywhere in the country. I wasn't necessarily set on going far. I was only set on going.

I made myself useful and helped my parents with the move. Aside from a few paintings and keepsakes, my father's main claim was the leather couch. He'd slept on that couch every night for ten years. He slept on his back, his hands folded over his round stomach like a soldier, or a corpse. It was normal for him to be overtaken by coughing fits. He smoked two packs of cigarettes a day.

João helped my father and me mount the couch onto the back of his pickup truck. The two of them rode together. I trailed behind them in a separate car with the rest of my father's belongings. I stared at that couch all the way to Nico's house. My mother and father had bought the couch, made of a smooth brown leather, when they had first arrived in the United States. Decades later, the couch remained in good shape. My parents referred to the couch as New York. They had a chunk of money set aside to take a trip there, but decided to buy the couch instead.

When my father was home, he was on the couch. In the evening, he watched the news. At night, he watched movies. On the weekend, he watched sports. I watched a lot of television with my father. We talked about what we watched. The news, mostly, and sports. But every now and then he'd get drunk and we'd talk about other things. His marriage to my mother, for example. The marriage hadn't worked out for several reasons, although the fundamental one was that his mother-in-law had always made my mother feel guilty about leaving Colombia.

There's a distinct image I have of my father from my childhood. It's five o'clock in the morning and he's holding a quart-sized mug full of black coffee. He has a cigarette between his teeth. He sets the mug down to button his collared shirt and to tie his tie. He's red-faced, sweaty, and breathing heavily. He tucks his shirt into his underwear, classic white briefs, then pulls his slacks up to his belly. When he kisses me before leaving, he leaves me smelling like his cologne.

We were off the highway, on the backroads that led to Nico's former house, my father's future home. I thought about my father's phone call with my sister a few weeks before. I had been in my room upstairs when I heard him screaming about some usual subjects. Money, debt, and a lack of gratitude. How she'd missed my graduation and Nico's funeral. Silently, I watched him. He was on the couch, leaning over the coffee table. His voice softened. He said he had lost many people in his life, for good, and explained that he had always found a way to keep going. He pulled the phone away from his ear mid-sentence. Ana had hung up. He dropped the phone and took a sip of rum, then slammed the glass on the table. Glass shattered in all directions. As I helped him gather the pieces, blood began to leak from his lip onto his teeth. He took a minute to speak.

"I am going to die soon," he said, "and when I do you will be the only friend I have."

"That's not true," I said.

"It's okay if it is," he said.

It took weeks to sort through my mother's belongings. These were good, busy weeks. My mother slept in the king-sized bed they'd once shared. I'd always been confused by the way she took up only half the mattress. I thought she should've slept in the middle. But she kept to her side, and when she slept, she slept closer to the edge than she did to the center.

When she wasn't sleeping and wasn't making all of our lives easier, she kept busy in the small study adjacent to her bedroom. She'd sit in her rocking chair by the window, reading novels and self-help books. She'd sit at her computer and catalogue her photographs. More than anything, she was fond of organizing her belongings, of ordering and reordering the material and emotional accumulation of the life she had and had not lived. It was when I helped my mother pack for her move to Colombia that I was able to envision what her life could've been.

She cried as we went through all of the schoolwork she'd collected from Ana and me. She was proud of the fact that she'd kept everything we'd produced when we were younger:

the drawings, the paintings, the crafts, the many worksheets that listed our goals and dreams. My mother couldn't bring herself to take them out to the trash. And so I did.

She didn't cry when we unboxed the many binders she had filled as a software engineer, and she didn't cry when we threw them away. Together we flipped through the loose-leaf papers of her education. She was no older than twenty-five, had only been in the United States for two or three years, when she was accepted to a good university. She graduated at the top of her class. She had the notes to prove it. Each binder was filled with perfect handwritten coding. My mother lamented the fact that she hadn't studied what she'd wanted to study. She regretted what many people regret most: listening to someone else when she could've listened to herself. She'd wanted to be an interpreter, to work at an embassy, or a court, or a school. She'd wanted to be a bridge between worlds. That's how she put it.

There was one thing my mother demanded that I understand. She repeated it to me every chance she had. "Many people say that life is short. They're wrong. Life is long," she would say, "life is very long."

She collected couples. Little statue pairs made of glass, wood, or stone. I'd always thought the collection was pretty sad. Especially when my mother would tell me, from the time I was ten or eleven years old, how badly she wanted to be on her own, how tired she was of resenting my father and being resented by him. Still, she never said she regretted any of it. It was when she decided to keep them all, those couples, that I understood why she'd ever started collecting them in the first place.

She left in August. The night before she left, she asked me if I was going to be okay. I told her I didn't think anyone was going to be okay. We both laughed. She gave me a small purple stone. She told me it would give me direction.

"Take it with you wherever you go," she said.

Ana hadn't been to the house in years, but she always had a room. One night, after some argument she'd had with my father, Ana and I ended up in her bathroom. We drank and smoked for hours. I sat in the empty bathtub and she sat on the toilet. She told me that both she and my mother could see the future in their dreams. This was news to me. It might've been true. All the women on my mother's side of the family had always spoken to each other in their own language, one which I wasn't allowed to learn. That night, Ana told me about the times, when I had been very young, when she and my mother would pretend that I wasn't there. They pretended not to see or hear me. According to my sister, I'd scream at them and they wouldn't even acknowledge it. Out of frustration, I would knock things over and squirt dish soap all over the floor. "It's a ghost," they'd say.

We ended up drinking three bottles of cheap wine between the two of us. After finishing two, my sister vomited into the toilet on which she'd been sitting. I thought the night was over and told her we should go to sleep. She laughed, brushed her teeth, and then sat back down to resume our night, our drinking, and our smoking. She proceeded to reminisce about other drinking episodes, times when friends had fallen and split their heads open, and others when they'd fallen asleep on park benches.

I borrowed a line from our parents and asked if all the drinking wasn't expensive. Her laughter turned bitter. We landed awkwardly on the subject of her large debts. "Money isn't real," she said. When I asked her how that made any sense, Ana shook her head. "I won't be around to pay it," she said.

The sun was beginning to rise and Ana's train to the airport would leave in a few hours. I asked what the future held, what her dreams had shown her. Ana said I was going to be okay, that she might not be, and that she was going to disappear until she was better or until she wasn't. "The way all good animals do," she said.

I kept some of the family photographs.

João and my father had been friends for years. When João would come over, they'd sit at the kitchen table and share coffee and cigarettes. João looked like a young version of my father. He was always talking about his family, his wife, his daughter, and his infant son. He was always thanking God.

While we were moving out of our house, João and his family were moving into another. He'd just rented a house on the edge of a large property owned by a man he worked for. It was an old red barn that had been falling apart for years. João was rebuilding it. He was doing it all himself. He was happy. He talked about how safe his children were in their new home, the good schools they'd be able to go to in the fall, how lucky they all were. Aside from age, the only real difference between João and my father was that João worked with his hands and my father worked with his computer. That, and João didn't have papers.

João and his family inherited everything my family no longer needed. He kept the dining room set, my mother's bed, my sister's bed, my bed, and some other furniture. One Sunday, João's wife, Adriana, came over and picked out a couple of paintings my mother had left behind: parrots in the Amazon, couples kissing in the rain. She brought her children. They inherited the toys and video games my sister and I had grown up with.

Adriana and João invited us over to their new home. Before they walked us in, they apologized for not having finished rebuilding it. I'd never seen such a beautiful house. João had repainted the outside a bright red. It sat on the edge of an open field, like a painting or a postcard. João and Adriana, their children, and his mother welcomed us at the door. They showed us everything they'd inherited from my family. With his own hands, João had installed a kitchen, a bathroom, a room with desks for his children to do schoolwork, a bedroom for him and Adriana, one for his mother, and another for his two children. I asked João how they did it. He told me he hadn't been sleeping. Every day he and Adriana would go to work. She cleaned houses. He built them. Every night, Adriana would take care of the children and her mother-in-law. He would stay up building the house they lived in. "God is everything," he said.

My father took time off work to finalize the move. For two weeks, we emptied what'd been left over. For two weeks we cleaned. It wasn't exactly hard work. Every night or so we'd drink rum and smoke and talk until he fell asleep. I would make sure he was on his side with a glass of water in reach, then I would sit in all our empty rooms.

In the mornings, we'd watch the news. The election was coming. It wasn't much different from watching reality television with Nico. I guess it was more terrifying. More entertaining as well. My father lectured me about politics. "Blood sport," he called it. Trump was everywhere. The wall, the swamp, lock her up, et cetera. My father didn't think he'd win. Wishful thinking, I guess. I didn't know what to expect.

One morning, I asked my father what he thought of Washington. He said he wouldn't want to live there, but that he liked to visit. The few times he'd been, he felt like he was being watched everywhere he went. Too much bureaucracy. Too many politicians. Too many cops. But he loved the museums. "They're free," he said. He went on to say he had read somewhere in the Colombian news that a Botero exhibition was going to take place at one of the museums. Paintings of Abu Ghraib.

"It might be worth going," I said.

My father agreed. In a way, he seemed excited for me. "If you want to go, you should," he said. "You are young. You have nothing to lose. Whatever happens, wherever you go in the world, you are always welcome back."

I asked if it wouldn't be dangerous, considering the election and all that came with it.

He shrugged. "It's an important election. As important as they get." He laughed a little. "As they say, *May you live in interesting times.*"

I imagined myself roaming the museums each day. I imagined working them, at night, the way Nico had when he had been young and happy. I told my father I wanted to go and see if I liked it. He warned me. He told me that the universe was indifferent, that money was safety, that no one was welcome anywhere without it. He offered to give me some so, as he put it, I wouldn't make a mess. I accepted.

September came. My father and I were at the train station. I told him I was worried about him being alone with all of our ghosts. "The ghosts were here first," he laughed. I thanked him. He told me not to cry. He told me to go.

PART TWO

MAGDALENA'S HOUSE

I stayed in a hostel for a week, in Adams Morgan, by all the bars and clubs and hookah lounges. The receptionists were kind enough to let me pay night by night while I looked for a more permanent living situation. I received a keycard, a sleep mask, shampoo, a toothbrush, toothpaste, a towel, and a lock and key for my valuables. I was assigned a bottom bunk on the second floor, across the hall from the men's bathroom. The quarters were tight, but clean. The room was empty when I arrived. Some bunks were a mess, littered with clothes, chargers, maps, and pamphlets. Others were a bit tidier. I took my spot in the back corner, by the window, slid my luggage under my bunk, and slept through the evening, through the night, and into the weekday morning. I woke up as the more serious types buttoned up for work. I followed them downstairs into the communal kitchen and a complimentary continental breakfast. I reminded myself that I was lucky and returned to my bed for more sleep.

In the afternoon I walked, but not far. I walked through Columbia Heights, Shaw, and Dupont. The hostel guests mainly fell into two groups: tourists and professionals. The tourists wore backpacks and the professionals wore nametags. They were easy to tell apart on weekdays. On the weekends, they blurred together. They drank. They talked. They laughed. They fought. And so on.

Every day, and most nights, I ate at a small empanada restaurant in Adams Morgan, about a block away from my lodging. The empanadas weren't the best I'd ever had. They weren't the worst, either. The woman at the counter was very nice. One night, I asked her if she was the one who made all the empanadas. She laughed and pointed to the name on the door. "Julia makes them." I took my time eating. Every now and then the woman at the counter would run back into the kitchen or out for a quick errand. She would ask me if I would look after the counter while she was gone, which I did. It felt good to be trusted. I sat at the table by the window while I waited for her to return. I basked in the feeling, however slight, of being welcome.

One night, a Saturday, I was having a hard time sleeping. I was in and out of dreams for hours. Despite my earplugs, I could hear some guests singing downstairs. Later on in the night, I woke to a couple having sex on the other side of the dark room. I remember wishing I were both of them. It must've been three or four in the morning when I was woken up for the last time. The woman on the bunk above me was praying.

The morning after, I waited around for someone in the lobby to leave their Sunday paper behind, then brought the news back to bed with me. I came across an article about an unlikely, yet practical, living arrangement that was becoming more and more common. Many older folks needed younger people to help them with the tasks of daily living, and many young people needed affordable rent.

I was almost finished with the article when two members of the cleaning staff walked into my room. One mopped the floors while the other replaced the sheets in each empty bed, mine being the only one still occupied. I pretended to read while I listened to them speak in Spanish. They both agreed that their children were growing up too fast, especially their daughters. The women worked quickly. They were breathing heavily.

"I'm thirsty," said the woman mopping.

The woman responsible for bedding was on the top bunk, above me. She spoke as if she were speaking to no one, or God. "What year is it?" she joked.

Using a computer at the hostel, I found a listing for a basement apartment in Georgetown. It'd been posted two days prior by a recently widowed Spanish woman who needed help keeping up with her house. The listing called for a young male Spanish speaker with a clean background and, preferably, experience with home maintenance and yardwork. I didn't exactly qualify but called the listed number anyway. The woman's name was Magdalena.

"What's your name?" she asked.

"Gregorio," I said.

Magdalena spoke in perfect English and perfect Spanish, though she never mixed the two. Her Spanish was a harsh Spanish, from Spain, and therefore foreign to me. Her English was much milder. I couldn't detect any accent at all. Magdalena sounded like any American mother in the town where I'd been raised. She spoke, it seemed, with the voices of two people.

Over the phone, Magdalena gave me a very brief history of her life. She'd been born in a small city in the north of Spain. She'd recently lost her husband to, as she put it, old age. She needed some help around the house. She didn't like to be alone.

"Don't you have family?" I asked.

"No," she said.

"What exactly *is* the job?"

"Your job would be to make my life a little easier," Magdalena said. "That's all."

"What does it pay?"

"A room of your own."

"I can help," I said. Magdalena asked me to tell her a little bit more about myself over the phone before we met for a formal interview. I told her the truth. I told her that I was new in town and that I was far from home.

I was early for my interview. Magdalena was late. I sat waiting at a small table on the shaded patio of the specialty market in Georgetown. I was surrounded by expensive dogs and their owners. When asked what I would like, I ordered two cups of coffee and a small loaf of bread.

Magdalena arrived wearing a gray cashmere sweater to match her silver hair. She was contained, yet warm. She said hello as if we'd already met and shook my hand with both of hers. She was as attractive as anyone I'd ever talked to. Magdalena took one sip of her coffee, put the mug down, and asked the waiter for two glasses with ice.

She removed a notebook and pen from her tote bag. "Where is home?" she asked.

"Danbury," I said.

"Danbury?" she asked, unsatisfied.

"Danbury, Connecticut," I repeated.

"And your parents?"

"Colombia."

"Ah," Magdalena said, nodding. She set her notebook down and poured the lukewarm coffee into the cup with ice. I did the same. I noticed that there was no writing in her notebook, only scribbles of cubes across the page.

"I've never been to Colombia," Magdalena said.

"There's a river there with your name," I said.

"I didn't know," she said, smiling. "Have you been?"

"To Colombia? Yes. To the river? No."

Magdalena asked about my family's history. I told Magdalena about my recent trip and Nico's death. She nodded as I spoke. My family's reasons for leaving Colombia were not simple, but they were obvious. Their story was a common story.

Magdalena's story was not as common. She managed, though, to tell it simply and calmly. She was from Guernica, born without grandparents or aunts or uncles or cousins. They had all been lost in the famous bombing of the town in 1937, at the beginning of the Civil War, when Franco let Hitler test his warplanes on their Basque rivals. Both Magdalena's mother and father were orphaned following the bombing. Both were teenagers. They were taken in and cared for by the same woman, Magdalena, who had tragically lost her own husband and children in the same bombing. Eventually, Magdalena passed. The two orphans kept her house. Years later, they had a daughter of their own. They named her Magdalena.

"How did you end up here?" I asked.

"I went to university in Madrid. I met an American studying abroad there. We ended up together. Then we moved here and married. Thirty-five or so years ago, now."

"The husband who died?"

"That one."

"I'm sorry," I said.

She laughed politely. "For what? You've done nothing wrong."

The interview lasted about two hours. Because of my age, nineteen, Magdalena was under the impression that I was a university student. I explained that I wasn't and didn't exactly plan on becoming one. She suggested I sit in on some classes anyway.

"Take your backpack with you and find a seat," she said. "You'll fit right in."

The only direct question Magdalena asked me was whether I had any experience with maintenance. I lied and said that I did, that I'd helped my uncle out with landscaping and some other work around the house.

She shrugged. "There isn't really much to do. The yard is small and the house is in good shape."

"Perfect," I said.

Before showing me the house, Magdalena needed to do a background check. Once that was clear, I could move in. I handed her my license. While Magdalena photographed it, I drew a few cubes of my own next to hers. Magdalena shook my hand once more. "See you soon," she said.

A basset hound tied with its leash to a patio table stared up at me as I stood to leave. The dog was unattended. It cried a little. I gave it half of my loaf of bread. It swallowed the loaf in seconds, then continued crying. I gave the dog the other half and left.

I spent more time at the tourist spots than I should've. I like to think it was a necessary, or at least inevitable, mistake. It made me sad, or mad, or both, when I saw tourists taking pictures of themselves smiling beside war memorials, or in front of giant marble statues of slave-owning presidents. The Washington Monument was, as my father had joked many times, an erection. I realized that most monuments were erections, one way or another. And it became clear to me, after the sun had gone down and the tourists had dispersed, that someday the monuments would be ruins.

I sat at the World War II memorial and smoked. I sat with my back against a marble pillar and listened to the water from the fountain. I grew tired and began to dread my walk back to the hostel. A man walked up to the fountain. He looked around, looked at me, and decided I wasn't a threat to whatever he was about to do. He began to undress. He stood in the fountain and bathed.

My background check was completed within a couple of days. Magdalena sent me an email confirming our arrangement. I was there the next morning. When I arrived, she was on the front steps of her red brick townhouse. She stood to greet me. "Welcome home," she said, and gave me a customary Spanish kiss on both cheeks.

Magdalena quickly showed me the small shed where she kept the standing mower, the bush clippers, and the trash bins, then took me into the house. The front door opened into a long, dark hallway. There was a tearoom that seemed to have been untouched for years. There were no photos either, only paintings of open fields and empty oceans. The chairs looked uncomfortable and weak. When I dusted the house a few days later, I could see that the seats were made of leather, each depicting an engraved image of a bullfight.

The dining room was not much different, though a bit brighter. At the head of the long wooden table, where Magdalena's husband once sat, was an empty linen placemat. Magdalena's placemat lay next to it. On it was a silver tray, a silver plate, and silver utensils. On the mantel by the window there was a miniature house statuette. The house looked familiar. I bent down to look closely. I realized it was the very house I was standing in. I liked it. I asked Magdalena who'd made it.

"I did," she said.

The living room consisted of a set of matching leather sofas, a rocking chair, and a huge television.

"Do you enjoy watching television?" I asked.

"Who doesn't?"

There were several paintings, drawings, and sketches hanging from the living room walls, all without color, each one seemingly incomplete and cut off from some larger whole. There was a horse's head screaming and crying, its eyes looking up at the sky. Another drawing presented a clenched fist around a broken sword. There was a lost bull, a crying man with outstretched arms, a light bulb, a ghost coming in through an open window, and a wailing mother holding a dead child. I must've been staring, because Magdalena spoke as if to answer a question she could read on my face.

"Guernica," she said.

Magdalena didn't show me to her bedroom, but she did walk me through the rest of the upstairs. Her office was small and littered with jewelry. I saw silver. I saw gold. Emeralds, too. There was a desk at the window facing the quiet Georgetown street. Velvet displays of her most important pieces were hung up on the walls. Magdalena seemed to have more gold than the Vatican. I asked her if she was related to the queen.

"This is where I work," she said.

Magdalena's late husband's office displayed various degrees. There was a brick of gold on the corner of his black wooden desk.

"He was a gold analyst," she said.

The basement apartment had everything I needed except its own entrance. There was a small kitchen with a refrigerator, a small table for two people, a full bathroom, a desk, and a pull-out couch. Magdalena was sorry that it didn't have any windows. I told her it was a good thing, that I would sleep well no matter what the weather was like.

"Get settled," Magdalena said. "If you need anything, let me know."

"Likewise," I said.

I tacked old pictures of my family on the bathroom mirror. I placed Nico's letter, my mother's purple stone, and my father's money in the nightstand drawer. I got in bed, tried to sleep, and couldn't. I went for groceries. I bought bananas, cereal, eggs, pasta, rice, and beans. My cooking was limited. I would only make food when I was especially hungry. But I was rarely hungry.

That night I drank too much rum and vomited in the toilet. The next morning, Magdalena invited me up for breakfast. Eggs and bacon. She told me she'd heard me getting sick and asked if I was okay. I apologized.

"For what?" she asked.

She told me to eat slowly. The food helped, but it was the broth she'd boiled that really saved me. Magdalena reminded me to go to class. It was the beginning of September and the universities were starting up that week. I told her I'd go. I had nothing better to do. I did the dishes. I took out the trash.

INTRODUCTION TO ECONOMICS

I walked a few blocks uphill to the Georgetown campus and followed the youngest looking group of students into the largest lecture hall. My first class was an introduction to economics. There must've been at least two hundred people. The professor read the syllabus aloud. "The course," he said, "will introduce you all to the principles and policies affecting the economy, as well as to economic ethics." The professor emphasized that his goal was to teach us the language of economics so that we could speak it for the rest of our lives.

The next class I attended was Biology 101. The professor was more relaxed and more interesting. She had bright red hair and wore blue jeans and an oversized button-down shirt. The first thing she said about biology changed my life. She said that all species were destined to become extinct.

The last class I ever attended was an introductory chemistry class, taught by a tall Argentinian guy with a thick accent. I understood him perfectly. The class, he explained, was for non-majors, and therefore would not focus on the intricacies of chemistry but instead on the realities of the global climate disaster. "Many of you will go on to have big careers in business and politics. Most of you will have children. The future is coming, quickly, and it is crucial that you understand the circumstances that will dictate everything. In short, the objective of this course is for you to understand that the world is ending. Climate change is real and irreversible. It is already too late." The lecture hall was quiet. The professor proceeded to pull up the syllabus on the projector. He said that the class would be easy so long as students attended regularly. He assigned one textbook. He'd written it himself.

Outside the lecture hall, by the bathroom, there was a bulletin board with fliers advertising different opportunities to make money. I took a couple of them with me. The first was for smokers between the ages of eighteen and twenty-four. The second was a family dynamics survey. The third was a sleep surveillance study.

First, I showed up to the smoking study. They assumed I was a student and asked what class I wanted credit toward. I told them that I wasn't a student. When they asked me why I was interested in participating, I told them I wanted to make myself useful, and that I wanted to make money. There was more paperwork than I expected. The woman in charge of carrying out the study asked me a series of questions. She asked me how often I smoked, why I smoked, and whether I was trying to quit or not. I told her I smoked half a pack a day, that I smoked because I enjoyed smoking, and that I did not plan to quit. She explained that the study was designed to measure the extent to which cigarette packaging affected young smokers. She asked to see my pack, which had one warning: *Smokers Die Younger.*

My job was to transfer my cigarettes into the packs the study provided and keep a tally of how many cigarettes I smoked each day. The pack she gave me was plain cardboard with warnings on both sides. One side had a picture of an aging smoker hooked up to an oxygen tank, surrounded by what appeared to be his devastated family. The other side had a picture of a stillborn baby. I was required to report back once a month over the course of the study, where I would be asked a series of questions about my experience. I would get paid each time I reported back.

The Family Dynamics Survey people weren't interested in my participation. They asked me if I had a child with a partner I was living with. I said I didn't, but that I was willing to contribute to the study anyway. They said that I was useless to them. When I asked why and told them I had a lot to say about family dynamics, they told me that the study was designed to see if there was a correlation between the amount of sleep a child gets and the parents' satisfaction with their relationship. I asked them how they planned to measure satisfaction. "Satisfaction is self-reported," they said.

The sleep surveillance people were very excited to see me. They weren't as excited when I told them I wasn't a student. I'm not sure why. I assume it's because they'd have to pay me, or because they thought I wouldn't be as reliable. Probably both. Still, they had me fill out all their paperwork. They were concerned that I hadn't been to a doctor in years.

I was required to wear a home sleep tester every night for two weeks. The device was impressive. There was a nose tube to measure my breathing, a belt that I had to wrap around my chest to measure more breathing, a finger clip to measure the oxygen in my blood, and a position sensor to record when I was asleep on my back, side, or stomach. I didn't ask too many questions, only why they were studying people's sleep. They said that sleep problems helped cause heart disease, depression, and poor work performance. I wondered if heart disease, depression, and poor work performance caused sleep problems, but I didn't say anything. I was to be paid at the end of the study, after I'd reported back with the sleep machine and completed an exit interview with the staff.

When Magdalena asked me how class had gone, I told her I'd gotten three jobs instead. I showed her the pack from the smoke study and the sleep machine. When I told her how much I was getting paid, she joked that she was going to sign up, too.

"I should start smoking again," Magdalena said.

"It's never too late," I said.

That night I made pasta for the two of us. It wasn't good, but Magdalena said it was. The best part of the dinner was the wine. The conversation was nice, too. Magdalena asked what I was planning on doing for work, if anything. I told her I'd been thinking about working at one of the museums, as a janitor maybe. I explained that my uncle Nico had done the same when he was my age at a Botero museum in Medellín.

"Which museum do you want to work at?" she asked.

"I don't know," I said. "Which one do you recommend?"

"None of them," Magdalena said. "What you *should* do is go to school."

"I should," I said. "You're right."

"I am right," she said.

"Will you pay?" I asked. Magdalena laughed. We opened a second bottle of wine. Magdalena stole a cigarette from my pack.

"What would you study?" she asked.

I made a point to look around at the house. "Gold," I said, laughing. I asked Magdalena what she studied at university.

She grew a little sad. "General courses. I never finished. I only studied a year."

"If you go to school, I'll go to school," I said.

"Deal," she said.

That night we watched a television documentary about the Vietnam War. Magdalena and I fell asleep next to one another on the couch. I woke up, turned everything off, and went downstairs to my apartment. I wrote down that I'd smoked fifteen cigarettes, then hooked myself up to the sleep tester and went to bed. That night I dreamed that Nico and Magdalena were young. They sat across from one another in a small room without windows. They talked for hours. When I woke up, I couldn't remember what they'd said.

SMITHSONIAN

The National Gallery of Art was massive and overcrowded. There were too many priests. There were too many saints. Too many naked women, and Jesuses. I liked the East Building a bit better. There was a painting of a barefoot family standing on a blue beach, Picasso's *The Tragedy*. Nobody in the painting was speaking. The mother and father were looking down, or away. The boy held his hands out, as if he'd asked them a question they couldn't answer. There was a photography exhibit by Carrie Mae Weems, *The Kitchen Table Series*. There was a guard in the corner. He was bald and he was writing in a small notebook. I wanted to ask him what he was writing. I wanted to know if he was writing poems, letters, stories, or if he was just making a list. I stared at a picture of a man and a woman eating dinner at a kitchen table. The man had finished his dinner and was having his beer. On his plate there was a small mound of lobster shells. The woman's wine glass was full, the lobster on her plate whole, its claws rubber-banded.

I asked about a guard job at the front desk. They told me they didn't need guards. They gave me the phone number of the janitorial company that maintained the museums and wished me luck.

I wasn't particularly interested in the Museum of Natural History. I never set foot in the Museum of American History or the National Archives. I didn't go to the Air and Space Museum either. I felt comforted by the immensity of the universe and how small the world was in comparison. What I wasn't interested in was conquering the unknown.

One evening, around closing time, I ended up at the Museum of the American Indian. There was a concert going on in the atrium. People sang. People danced. Part of me wanted to sit in the front row. I walked up the corridor that wrapped itself upward, toward the top of the building. I leaned over the edge on the second floor and watched until the concert ended.

On my walk home, I passed by an apartment building surrounded by cop cars. The sidewalk was blocked off with police tape. On the pavement there was a small pool of blood. Aside from the cops, there were a few people standing around. Some of them cried. Most were quiet. I asked a woman who wasn't crying what had happened. She told me that the ambulance had just left, that someone had tried suicide by jumping from a window on the top floor. When I asked if the person had died, she said no, that they'd hit a tree on the way down and it'd broken their fall. I tried sleeping and ended up drinking instead. The next day I woke up on the bathroom floor with the broken sleep tester tangled around my neck.

THE PORTRAIT GALLERY

The only maintenance job available was a night position at the National Portrait Gallery, located between Chinatown and the White House. They hired me to take care of the trash and the recycling. It was only a couple of nights a week to start, but I was told it would turn into more if I did a good job. I filled out the paperwork and the boss gave me a keycard to the building and the janitor's closet. I got paid every other week.

There was a lot of trash. More than I expected from a museum. I had to take care of bathrooms, offices, hallways, stairways, exhibits, meeting rooms, entrances, exits, and the gift shop. The smell wasn't so bad. The hardest part was taking the trash bags out to the dumpster. A full bag would suction itself to the bottom of the container. I learned to be inefficient. When the container was halfway full, I'd take it out to the dumpster. I took my time. The more time I took, the more I got paid.

The employees' offices varied, though not much. Some of their desks were so organized it seemed like they didn't have anything to do. Others consisted of stacked folders and documents, topped off with little yellow reminders. There was an important photograph on almost every desk. There were wedding photos, family portraits where everyone wore the same shirt, and pictures of babies with food on their faces. It was strange to be alone in a room at night where someone else had been alone all day. I enjoyed it.

There were entire sections of the museum where I tried to keep my head down as I passed through. I did my best to ignore the Civil War, the treasure maps for colonists, the portraits of settlers. I tried to do the same with the presidents. There were bronze and marble statues of the early ones' faces. Washington and Lincoln, for example. It was like they'd been beheaded and preserved. As for the others, I guess the only difference between the paintings was whoever had been paid to paint the portrait. Some were more abstract than others. Some looked at me as I walked by. Others gazed upward. They all looked the same to me. They'd all sat in the same chair. They'd all presided over the same empire.

After two weeks of trash, I was promoted to bathrooms. I didn't mind. I mopped the floors, disinfected the baby changing tables, cleaned the mirrors, emptied the tampon bins, bleached the toilets, replaced the toilet paper and the hand soap. If Magdalena ever needed anything for her bathrooms, I was able to bring it to her for free. I'd restock the house's bathrooms without a word. Every now and then she'd make a joke about the perks of my new job.

"You're quite the provider," she once said.

I enjoyed the museum's bathrooms. I'd look at what people had written on the stalls: insults, puns, hearts with dates and names. My favorite was inscribed in a men's room stall on the first floor: "If you build it, they might come."

After about a month of bathrooms, they gave me my own wing to clean. I was told it was a promotion, even though the pay was the same. My job was to vacuum the carpets and mop the tiles. They started me out on the third floor. At the time, they were setting up a Fernando Botero exhibit. It hadn't yet been opened to the public, though the installation left its own dusty mess. They didn't have any of his sculptures. Instead, he'd loaned them his paintings of Abu Ghraib. There was one of men behind bars piled on top of one another, each one of them gagged, tied, and blindfolded. There was another of a naked, bleeding man hung upside down by one foot. A soldier pissing on a naked prisoner's back. A prisoner being waterboarded. An open hand suspended by a rope, tied around a bleeding wrist.

One of my other favorites was Nam June Paik's *Electronic Superhighway*. It was a mural that stood floor to ceiling, made up of different sized televisions. There was a red line between the map and me, and a voice that repeated "PLEASE STAND BACK" when I got too close. I'd sit in front of that map every now and then. D.C. was the smallest. You had to get close to really see it. There was one of those handheld televisions and a camera lens pointing right at me. I got so close that all I could see was myself, and all I could hear was "PLEASE."

The Throne of the Third Heaven of the Nations' Millennium General Assembly was the most beautiful chair I'd ever seen. According to the museum's description, the artist referred to himself as Saint James Hampton. He was a janitor, unmarried and childless. He'd collected the most beautiful garbage he could find: tin foil, lightbulbs, purple cardboard, old glass jars. From trash, he built a throne for Christ's return to earth. It was the only thing he'd ever made. The throne hadn't been finished. After Saint James died, someone found it in a garage he'd rented for fourteen years. As far as anyone knew, he'd worked on it in total privacy until his death.

The central throne sat in the middle of the platform. There were pulpits and mercy seats, pedestals, plaques, and altars. Two words were written at the head of the throne: "Fear Not." Next to the altar, in a glass case, was the book he'd hand-written in a language he'd invented. A language between himself and God. The same words were written at the bottom of each page: *Revelation.*

One night I climbed onto the platform. Saint James had inscribed a citation on the cardboard crown: *Hurt not the earth, neither the sea, nor the trees, till we have sealed the servants of our God in their foreheads.* In his notebook, Saint James wrote: *This is true that the great Moses the giver of the tenth commandment appeared in Washington, D.C., April 11, 1931.* He'd also written about Mary: *This is true that on October 2, 1946, the great Virgin Mary and the Star of Bethlehem appeared over the nation's capital.*

Every night, after I'd finished all my cleaning, I'd sit before *The Throne.* I thought of James Hampton's twin callings, his art and his work. I imagined him walking to his job and seeing Moses. I imagined him walking home, fifteen years later, and seeing Mary and the Star of Bethlehem. I imagined him alone. Alone, with God.

Christ, I thought, must have already returned to earth. I wondered why Saint James, after all he'd done, hadn't been lucky enough to see Him.

FEAR NOT

I'd never felt better. I'd never mattered less. I spent most of my time at the museum. I enjoyed sitting by *The Throne*, regardless of whatever people would say when they looked at it. They said Saint James must've been crazy. They said he must've been a serial killer, and so on. I'd bite my tongue. Once or twice, I tasted blood.

Electronic Superhighway was always crowded. Typically, people would be most fascinated by whatever state they were from. They took a lot of pictures. Of themselves, mostly. There was a man who always happened to be sitting on one of the benches no more than ten feet away from the installation, staring at the screens but not one in particular, as if he were staring into a void. I loved the way he sat there, as if it were his own living room, as if he didn't mind who came to visit so long as they eventually left him alone. There was something honest about the way he'd decided to surround himself with televisions.

I'd sit on one bench and the man would sit on the other. There was never a word between us. I'm not sure if he ever noticed me. In all that time, he never looked away from the screens. When the museum's loudspeakers announced that it was closing for the night, he would wait to be escorted out by one of the security guards. As far as I knew, he'd come right back when the museum opened in the morning.

One night, after they'd left him out on the marble steps, I told him to follow me back inside. He didn't say anything, but he didn't hesitate to come with me. I snuck him in through one of the back doors. A security guard caught me sneaking him in. The first time I ever heard the man speak was when he told the security guard that I hadn't done anything wrong, that he'd followed me into the museum without me knowing.

The security guard told my supervisor. My supervisor called our boss. Our boss told my supervisor to take my keycard and send me home. He called me a week later to tell me that I was, in fact, fired. He told me to expect my final paycheck in the mail.

Magdalena was still awake when I got home from my last night of work at the museum. She was on the couch, watching the news, drinking red wine. "You're home early," she said.

"I lost my job," I said.

"What happened?" Magdalena asked, making space for me to sit next to her.

I gave Magdalena a long answer, much of which she'd already heard in the nights and weeks before. I told her about the museum, about the tourists, the bathroom graffiti, the televisions, and *The Throne*. She filled a glass of wine and put it in my hand.

"Why did you get fired?" Magdalena said, stopping me.

I explained that I'd let a man back into the museum after the security guard had kicked him out.

"Oh," Magdalena said sighing, "you can't do that."

"I won't let it happen again," I said.

Magdalena let out a small laugh. "You know," she said, "you can probably do better."

I shrugged and nodded. I asked for more wine. Magdalena filled my glass again and moved her hand up and down my back, her fingers touching the skin of my neck.

A boy's mugshot appeared on the television. Angel Morales had been arrested and charged with the first-degree murder of a college student in the area. A shooting. The news mentioned that the Angel was undocumented and that the murder was suspected to be gang related. I felt Magdalena looking at me without turning to me.

"Gregorio," she said, "are you documented?"

"Yes," I said bluntly. "My parents, too." In the background, the news moved onto the upcoming election. "What if I wasn't?" I asked.

Magdalena thought for a moment. I like to believe she answered honestly. "I think I would help you," she said.

"Good," I said.

Magdalena turned the television off after the news ended but didn't move from the couch. We split what was left of the wine into two equal pours. She asked me for a cigarette. She asked me about *The Throne*.

I told her everything I knew about it, and everything I knew about James Hampton. I told her what he'd written about Moses and Mary, and Christ's return to earth.

Magdalena nodded solemnly as I spoke. "Let me know if you see him," she said. Magdalena said goodnight to me with a kiss on the cheek and told me to sleep well.

The next day I worked around the house. I took care of all the dead leaves in the yard. I mopped the floors and dusted the blinds. I washed my dirty clothes and dirty sheets. Magdalena didn't leave her bedroom all morning. I began to worry and knocked. My excuse was that I was coming to get her dirty clothes and whatever else she might need me to clean.

"Come in," Magdalena said.

She was wearing a white robe. I could hear the water running for a bath. I gathered her clothes from the hamper and the sheets and pillowcases from her large bed. I worked quickly so as not to overstay. I was leaving with the dirty laundry when Magdalena called out from the open bathroom door.

"Don't work too hard," she said.

I took Magdalena's advice. There were nights when I walked around Georgetown, watching the other kids my age stumble in the streets. Sometimes I saw them fight. Sometimes I saw them vomit. I wouldn't say I was happy to watch these people unravel, not at all, but I couldn't look away.

Once, I walked by a crowded college bar. Someone asked me for a cigarette and talked to me about how she wasn't very impressed with the guys she went to school with. She said they were all spoiled, that they were all boys. She said that she wanted a real man, one with dirt underneath his fingernails. When I told her that I had just been fired from my janitor job at the museum, she thanked me for the cigarette and went back into the bar. Later that night, I overheard a conversation between three or four guys. One of the guys asked the others if they'd rather have sex with a woman without arms or a woman without breasts. They all agreed that a women's breasts were more important than her arms.

I thought of everyone I'd known in high school. Friends, teammates, classmates. I imagined them in equivalent campus bars across the Northeast, taking shots and pictures. I hadn't thought much about any of them since graduation, and I was sure they hadn't thought about me. I realized I might not see any of them again. With that thought came relief.

Another night, I ended up sitting and smoking with a man in front of the convenience store. He said I looked like someone who'd been in a couple of fights. I'd never been in a fight, but I took the compliment. He did most of the talking. He showed me this binder he'd been carrying around with him. Inside was an elaborate plan he'd devised to get money back from the government for a time he'd been wrongfully arrested in Texas. He told me they owed him millions of dollars, and that there was a government fund he was going to tap into. He went on about it for a while. I wished him the best of luck. I told him he could spend the night on my floor if he wanted to. He said no. He had a friend who worked maintenance at one of the hotels nearby who was usually able to sneak him into a room for the night.

A few times I ended my night by the canal. I'd let my feet hang off the footbridge and stare into the standing water. I'd re-read Nico's letter. It was during those long nights, when I paced around that strange city, that I learned that everyone was looking for something everywhere they went. I should've known that sooner, I suppose, but I didn't.

RAÚL'S CORNER

It was Election Day, a holiday for some. Magdalena voted by mail weeks before. I voted in person, on foot, at the local library. When I left the house that morning, Magdalena told me to be safe. I submitted my ballot then walked along the Potomac. I passed Watergate, the methadone clinic, the office buildings downtown and the people who hung from ropes as they washed them. I passed the White House and its black fence. Toward Chinatown, again. I read the war protest signs and surveyed the blanketed people holding them. I watched the families posing for pictures by the fence and the armed guards. People wore blue. Even more wore red. America was going to be great, again.

I walked up the museum's white marble steps and through the revolving doors. I thought about tax money. I bypassed the Civil War, Reconstruction, and Jim Crow. I crossed paths with the presidents and couldn't tell one from another. I saw Abu Ghraib and television America. I watched an old couple stagger eastward and westward. I watched a girl cross the line and trigger the automated warning. "PLEASE STAND BACK." I asked myself if free entry was worth the price of admission. I sat at the foot of Saint James' *Throne*. It was still empty.

I sat on the steps of the Portrait Gallery and watched as people walked by in all directions. Everyone seemed to be in some kind of hurry, as if they were late for something. Microphone voices came to me from around the corner. I decided to follow them, toward the corner of 7th and H, where the Chinese Friendship Archway stood next to the stairs that fed the Metro. There I stood on that crowded corner. Part of me wanted to move, to get out of the world's way. I told myself to get comfortable with the traffic behind me and the wind it threw at my back. To stand still and use my pockets. To stand in one place longer than I had to. To watch and witness.

Everyone talked. Some people screamed. The voices I'd heard before were the voices of six men and women crying into a microphone. They spoke of profit prisons, legalized murder, stolen land, and Judgment Day. They spoke of walls and policing and the Klan. They spoke of years and decades and centuries. I listened. A separate group shouted back. "Build the wall," they shouted, "Lock her up." Eventually they settled on chanting the initials of our country so loudly that the protesters couldn't be heard.

A gentle lady and a gentle man approached me with pamphlets and a sign that read: *Good News from God.*

"Is the Bible still relevant today?" they asked me.

"I don't see why not," I said.

When the student campaign interns asked me for a donation, I wished them good luck. When the balding optimist asked for my signature to help regulate campaign funding, I wished him good luck. When the man with the cigar told me to leave, to go back where I came from, I pretended not to understand and said nothing. Looking back now, I wish I had. When the toothless, sleepless woman asked me for five dollars, I gave her ten.

I stood on that corner until there was nothing left to be asked of me. It was then that I was able to lift my head, that I was able to see where I had planted my feet. Surrounded by technicolor. By chain stores, advertisements, and spokespeople. By discounts, guarantees, and tomorrows. Street vendors sold hats and t-shirts and statuettes, semen-colored Lincolns and semen-colored Washingtons. There were police on horseback and over-fed pigeons. Flags waving and teenagers dancing for cash.

I stood until I became invisible, more invisible than I'd ever been. Until all I could do for the world was know it well enough to wish it luck. I stood until I was tired, until I noticed.

A man reached out and handed me a menu for a Chinese restaurant nearby. I reached for it and thanked him. He'd been before me, with me, the whole time. He was maybe fifteen, twenty years older than me, with a gold chain tucked into the neckline of his thin jacket. He looked at me and grinned, as if there was nothing to say. As if to say, "Welcome."

I didn't know where he was from, but I knew he was from somewhere else. I didn't know anything about him other than what he looked like. What I knew is that he could've been my father, that his wife could've been my mother, that their sons and daughters could have been my brothers and sisters. On any other day, I would've thanked him and kept walking. I would've walked home, fried an egg, and slept well. But that day I was guessing my way through America. I was far from home, a place, I realize now, no longer even existed. I imagined my father watching the news on his old couch. I imagined my mother doing the same in Colombia, and my sister following along in Tucson. A great fear rooted itself in my stomach. To this day it has only grown. That

Election Day, on that corner, I realized this was not my country. It never would be. It never had been. And because I didn't know where else to go, I stood with him.

I wanted to tell the man this but knew better. I thought of the other Americas, the forgotten Americas, the Americas I'd known at a distance, the Americas my parents missed and did not miss. I thought of the wars he'd survived. I thought of the wars I'd slept through. I thought of bombs on buses and in plazas, kidnapped aunts and kidnapped uncles, dead journalists, dead candidates, and children at war. I thought of families so hungry they'd sold their children for food.

I began to write this man a story. I imagined him crossing a desert, an ocean, or a sky. I imagined him sending dollars to his family in hopes that they would join him, knowing he might never see them again. I imagined him sleeping alone and doing his job. I imagined him as he appeared before me: standing, holding onto menus in two languages that were not his, his living costing his boss less than an ad in the paper, costing less than a sign on the wall.

I asked myself what the difference was between an alien and an astronaut. I asked myself what the difference was between an invisible man and an invisible god. Before I left, I asked the man for his name.

"Raúl," he said.

I returned to *The Throne* with the menu Raúl had given me. The museum was empty, save the guards. I sat where I had sat so many times, before *The Throne*, and spoke. "This is true that Raúl, the second coming of our Savior, appeared in Washington, D.C. on November 8th, 2016."

And I sat before *The Throne* until I was asked to stand. And I prayed until I was forced to leave.

MAGDALENA'S KITCHEN ON THE
NIGHT OF THE ELECTION

I came back to a quiet home. The only light in the house came
from the kitchen. There, Magdalena sat with a bottle of wine.
Waiting, it seemed, for me.

"Gregorio," Magdalena said, "sit down."

I sat down and filled my glass.

"Where were you today?" she asked.

I tried the wine. It was red and bitter. "I walked to Chinatown."

"How was it?"

"Busy," I said, forcing a laugh.

Magdalena took a long sip. "Was it scary at all?"

"A bit," I said, "but most people were just doing their jobs.
Even God."

Magdalena raised her eyebrows. "Did you see him?"

I nodded.

"And what did he say?"

"His name," I said.

"That's good," Magdalena said. She took my hand and
pressed it between both of hers. She kept one palm to mine,
then ran the other over my fingers, my knuckles, and my wrist.

I could feel Magdalena's eyes on mine, reading me. I kept my eyes on our hands and, not knowing what else to say, waited for Magdalena to speak.

"When I was ten years old, I asked my mother if she believed in God. It was summer and we were in the garden behind our house. I already knew, at that age, about the bombing. How my mother and father had been orphaned by Franco's bombs. How this woman, this unbelievable woman, Magdalena, had taken my mother and father in. I knew the story and yet my mother told me the story again, there, in the garden. My mother said she didn't know why she'd survived. She said they'd found her in the rubble. She said that someone had heard her crying. It was said that God had saved her, that God had protected her. *Do you believe that, mother?* I asked her. She shook her head. *If that is true*, my mother said, *then it is also true that God dropped those bombs. If God is the reason I did not die*, my mother said, *then God is also the reason I was orphaned.*"

"Then what did you say?" I asked.

"Nothing," Magdalena said. "What would you have said, Gregorio?"

"Nothing," I said.

Magdalena continued. "My mother and father were political people. Not radical, but political. They had almost everything taken away from them. Almost. And so they worked hard to keep what they had left. Their Basque language, their Basque culture, they defended it. They organized. Were they terrorists? No. They were people trying to survive."

A tear ran down Magdalena's face and into the corner of her mouth.

"Trying?" I asked.

"I was twelve years old. It was 1968. Winter, I believe. If not winter, fall. The police broke into our home, in the middle of the night, and left with my parents. I remember their last words.

Both my mother and father said the same thing. *Run*, they said. I ran. I didn't get far. My parents, I found out later, were both executed the next day. Together, before a firing squad. I was relocated to an orphanage in Madrid, run by the Catholic Church. There, they took my language. They beat it out of me. They gave me a God to thank and a job to do. I cleaned. I cooked. And as soon as I was old enough, I left."

I held Magdalena's hands the same way she'd held mine.

"The only difference between you and me," Magdalena said, "the only important difference, the only difference that matters, is time. Time, and luck."

"Yes, Magdalena," I said.

"Do you understand what I'm saying, Gregorio?"

"I think so."

"We have a new tyrant, Gregorio. I have seen it happen. I have seen this movie before. This is not a new story. This is not a new story at all. This is a bad chapter, beginning. You are not safe. Your family is not safe. The world has not changed, Gregorio. I know what a tyrant can do. I might as well have been born yesterday, Gregorio. Do you understand?"

"Yes, Magdalena," I said, "I understand."

"Open another bottle," Magdalena said. "Can you do that for me?"

"Of course, Magdalena."

"And smoke, Gregorio. Smoke here with me. Light one for me, too."

"I can do that," I said.

"I don't want to be alone, Gregorio."

"Neither do I."

We talked long into that night about what to do next. I proposed that Magdalena leave, that she go somewhere else. She said Canada was too cold. Latin America in its entirety, for whatever reason, didn't feel like the right place, either. Spain, although it would always call her name, wasn't an option. "I feel at home here," Magdalena said, "for better and for worse."

Magdalena asked if I was scared for my family.

"Not so much," I said. "I'm more scared for our friends. For João, Adriana, and their children. And many, many others whose names I don't know."

"I understand," Magdalena said, nodding intently.

I shrugged. "I've been scared for them for a long time."

"Right," Magdalena said.

There was a silence. I said I wanted to do something, that I felt responsible. I explained that my parents had suggested, before I'd left them, to look into work as a translator or interpreter.

Magdalena liked the idea. She offered to help. "I know a place you can reach out to," she said.

"Who?" I asked.

"A church," Magdalena said, laughing a little, then yawning.

"Perfect," I said.

Magdalena fell asleep at the table. I helped her up from her chair and all the way to bed. I tucked her in. I couldn't tell if she was awake or if she was talking in her sleep. "Stay," she said. I stayed. Magdalena kept talking through her sleeping mouth. When she stopped, I slept.

KEEPING SCORE

I ended up with another job. This time I went to work at a small church in Columbia Heights, a community center on Spring Street that ran an after-school program for the neighborhood kids. They were looking for someone who could set a good example, speak both English and Spanish, and so on.

Grace was the one who interviewed me for the job. She was about my age, maybe a little older. She asked me to talk about my work experience, about my background, how good my Spanish was, whether I could speak it and read it and write it. I told Grace about my arrangement with Magdalena and my time at the museum. I told her that I could speak and read and write in Spanish, but that my English was a little better. Grace explained that none of their employees spoke any Spanish, even though most of the kids' parents couldn't speak English. She asked me to describe myself in three words.

"I'd rather not," I said.

Grace asked me if I had experience dealing with children. "Yes," I said, lying. Grace posed a hypothetical, an easy one. It was something about a mess. The question was whether I would go ahead and clean up as soon as I noticed one, or if I would wait for someone to tell me to do something about it.

"Clean it," I said.

"And your biggest weakness?" she asked.

"Sometimes I let people get away with things. Sometimes I look the other way," I said.

I was hired.

Dee Dee ran orientation. She was talking to everyone but she was looking right at me when she warned us. "Don't be soft with the kids," she said. "They're smart and they'll take advantage of your kindness if you let them." She went on to tell us, whether we believed so or not, that we had been chosen by God to be there.

I started a week later. On the way in I said hello to the pastor. He was pacing around in his nightgown, smoking a cigarette while he tossed breadcrumbs to the city squirrels. He did so every morning. I never could make out what he was saying, or whispering, to those squirrels.

The front doors were to remain locked at all times. "Always use the back door," Dee Dee said. "It'll be open between two thirty and two forty-five."

There were only a few rooms and there were only about twelve kids. That's all the church could afford. There was a small room for lunch next to the kitchen, an office with a couple of desks and one working computer, a playroom that we used for Bible study, a small parking lot out back where the kids could play games, a classroom where the kids supposedly did their homework, and the church itself, a modest Catholic chapel that was always empty.

When the parents had questions, Dee Dee and Grace would send for me. Sometimes the questions were simple. *What days are the kids going to the park? What time do the kids need to be picked up? How do I let the church know that my kid has permission to walk home alone?* And so on. They had other questions, questions I'd never answered before, responsibilities I didn't expect. *What does this immigration notice say? What day is the food bank open? Is there a doctor we can see?*

Once, Grace called me over to help one of the mothers fill out some paperwork. The mother told me that she had learned to speak some English, but still couldn't read or write. She smiled when she thanked me for my help. Several of her teeth were crowned with gold. She told me she was out of work and that she wanted to help clean the place. I told her I was sorry, that I was already in charge of maintenance. She said she would do it for free. That night I wept.

Sometimes they'd leave me in charge of the kids. It was a simple task. First, I had to make sure they didn't run away. Second, I had to make sure they didn't get hurt. Third, I made sure they were nice to each other. That's all you can really do. That's all I could really do, anyway. Every now and then Dee Dee would tell me I was too easy on them. "Yes, Dee Dee," I'd say, "you have a point."

Every day we played soccer in the parking lot. I found some old hockey nets in the custodian's closet and I'd set them out for the kids. I always played for whatever team was losing. The kids were set on keeping score. I guess I was the one with the bad habit of always making sure the game ended in a tie.

We did our best to organize a variety of activities. Gardening, for example. Dee Dee told us to use the small vegetable bed by the parking lot. When Grace and I took the kids out to introduce them to their new weekly project, the pastor rushed out of his house, in his robe. "Leave the plants alone," he said. I tried to explain that we were only going to show the kids how to water and tend to them, but he wouldn't listen. He said he didn't trust the children, so loudly that they could hear him.

I told Dee Dee that I thought pastors were supposed to be nice. "He must have a lot on his mind," she said.

Dee Dee had Grace and I lead arts and crafts activities. The girls preferred coloring. Enori and Erica seemed to always choose a cutout of a different Disney princess. They'd use different colors every time, funny ones. They gave the Little Mermaid green skin, blue hair, and even a little mustache. "Hey, mister," they'd say, "she looks just like you."

I told them not to call me mister, but they did it anyway. The boys did too. David would complain every time, saying he didn't want to color, that he didn't feel like doing anything. Eventually he started folding sheets of paper into guns. One time he pointed one of his guns at me. I got upset and made him throw it away. He refused to participate for the rest of the activity. The next day, he started making paper planes instead.

Julio preferred drawing. He was always drawing something. "What should I draw next?" he'd ask.

I usually told him to draw whatever he wanted, until one day he insisted I give him a prompt. "Why don't you do a self-portrait?" I said.

Ten minutes later he came back with a drawing of a boy whose body was made up of different sized squares, none of them touching one another, all of them spread out over the page and colored in with pencil. I liked it. I told him so. He agreed. "It's one of my stronger works," he said.

Bible study was every day. Miss Clara ran that. She had her own rocking chair. She even had her own room. It was small, but it was hers. I helped her set it up. She had me hide the toys. "If the kids see the toys," Miss Clara said, "they won't listen."

At first I'd sit through Bible study on the floor with my back against the wall, next to Grace. Miss Clara was always scaring the kids. She'd tell them that God was watching them, that He'd get mad at them if they didn't listen to her, or to me, or to Grace, or to Dee Dee, or to their parents, and so on. That's all she was ever really saying. My second week there, Miss Clara came up to me and said that she felt like she was finally starting to get through to the kids. I stopped going to Bible study. Grace stayed.

Instead, I'd help Dee Dee out in the kitchen. She was always cooking a second lunch for the kids in case they hadn't had enough at school, or in case they weren't going to have anything for dinner. Sometimes she really needed the help. Other times she seemed to enjoy my company.

The truth is the lunches weren't excellent. But they weren't bad, either. They were all donated. A truck brought them frozen every Monday. They were the kinds of lunches I used to get at school: frozen bagels, bagged ham and cheese sandwiches, canned beans, canned corn, frozen meatballs, frozen cheese sticks, apple sauce, and some other things. Dee Dee did what she could. She made pizza. We melted the cheese sticks on the bagels and used ketchup instead of tomato sauce. The kids were happy.

Dee Dee liked to talk about the daughter she'd had when she was too young, and the other two that she'd adopted later on in life. She said it was all part of God's plan for her, that He was testing her, and that I'd be tested too, someday. Whenever the food was ready, she'd call me over to try it out. I said the same thing every time. "Not bad, Dee Dee."

I'd leave the lunches out for the kids, that way they could come right back to them after Bible study. Before they could eat, though, I had to make sure all the boys washed their hands. Grace did the same for the girls. It was my job to stand in the bathroom with the kids to make sure they didn't do anything to each other.

That was the last thing I'd do every day before break. I ate alone. I'd make sure Grace was sitting with the kids and I'd go take my half hour. When Miss Clara was on her way in to lead prayer before lunch, I'd be on my way outside.

I circled the block every day. It was made up of old brick houses, each one divided into separate apartments. There was a soup kitchen a couple of houses down. Every time I passed by, I'd end up handing out two or three cigarettes.

By the time I got back I'd eat whatever I'd packed for lunch, usually a sandwich or a couple of bananas. I ate in the chapel. I'd sit cross-legged on the altar and eat my lunch until it was time to get back to work. Once, Grace found me while I was eating a banana. Half-laughing, she said that I looked like a monkey. "We're all monkeys," I said.

The chapel was the only place where I could be alone. Even when I locked myself in the bathroom stall, the kids would still find a way to talk to me. They would see my feet and laugh. "Hey, mister," they'd say, "you're taking a big dump."

"Yes, I am," I'd say. It didn't bother me. They laughed even harder when it hit the water. Julio told me that his mom would always get mad at him for clogging the toilet at home.

After lunch the kids were supposed to read. At first I tried to make them. That didn't work. So I read to them. I told them that a little bit of reading wasn't the worst thing they could do. One time I picked out a book, an illustrated one about the real history of Christopher Columbus' arrival to America, and read it aloud to a small group. It covered, among other things, his responsibility for the colonization, enslavement, and genocide of the native Caribbean people he had supposedly discovered. Miss Clara told me she wasn't sure if the kids were old enough to look through that one. I disagreed. In the end, Dee Dee decided to remove the book.

I found a picture book about Diego Rivera in a donation box and flipped through it with Julio. I told him that Rivera would make these huge paintings called murals, big enough so that anyone could come and see them. He looked through those pictures every day afterward. "Look," he'd say, "Diego Rivera."

Once the kids had finished reading, Miss Clara and Dee Dee would lead prayer. Then they'd make the kids sing religious songs I'd never heard before. I'd go ahead and clean up the bathrooms, put the nets away, take out the trash, and wipe down each room. There were a couple of times that I ended up staying late. I had nothing better to do. I took my time cleaning the kitchen and mopping the floors. I renewed the soap, the sanitizer, the toilet paper, and the paper towels. I organized the refrigerator and the freezer. I sat in the chapel once or twice. I liked to light the candles, then blow them out.

I did my job and the kids did theirs. They learned to trust me, I think. With that came a lot of crying. According to Grace, kids were just honest people.

Every afternoon David and his litter brother would walk in, silent. I'd try to get them to cheer up, but couldn't. One of them would start crying and then the other would, too. Once they cried for hours without stopping, their arms around one another the entire time. I'd tell them that they were good brothers, and they'd both nod and continue.

Sometimes Julio would cry too. He broke down one day because he'd gotten a question wrong on a quiz at school. He said he wasn't good enough.

"Good enough for what?" I asked.

"Anything," he said. I should've asked good enough for whom instead, but I sat with him until he stopped and left it at that.

Once, Dee Dee sent me to drop off some leftover carrots at the soup kitchen down the street. Someone had drawn a gang sign in the sand out front. I wiped it away with my feet. When I handed the carrots to a woman at the kitchen, she said that it was as if I'd brought a bag of diamonds.

Julio was the only one who ever got sick. One day, after lunch, he ran into the bathroom and threw up on the floor. Dee Dee took him to the office because we were afraid he might have something contagious. I went over to check on him and asked him how he was feeling.

"I throw up sometimes," he said.

"Yeah," I said, "it happens to me too." He helped me clean up.

One day he grabbed onto my arm and looked up at me and said, "You're my dad."

The kids were always losing their teeth. Sometimes their teeth fell out when they were eating lunch, sometimes they'd pull them out on their own. If I couldn't find a little baggy to put them in, I'd keep their teeth in my pocket until the end of the day.

The church ran a donation program that gave backpacks and school supplies to all the kids who needed them. Dee Dee called me into the office and told me to contact each kid's parents. She told me that in order for the kids to get the backpacks, each parent needed to prove that their kid received free lunch at school. I pretended to call. I approved each family on the list, one by one.

On an unusually warm day in December, I agreed to go play soccer with some of the kids after work. Grace told me not to worry about cleaning up, that she'd take care of it so I could go. On our way over to their house, I asked them what they wanted to be when they grew up. Julio said he wanted to be a teacher, or a doctor, or an artist. David and his brother said they wanted to be like their father. I asked them what their father did.

"He builds houses," they said.

Using a pair of discarded mattresses, Julio set up two goals in the little yard behind the house where all the boys lived. We played for about an hour or two. I put the boys on the same team against me. They won. Afterward, Julio's mother called us up to their apartment. She'd ordered pizza. We sat around the table and ate. I said goodbye to the boys and thanked Julio's mother for having me over.

"They're good kids," I told her.

"God bless you," she said.

The next day, Julio and his mother went to the church to speak with the pastor. Dee Dee called me through the two-way radio to help translate. Expecting the worst, I hurried over.

When I arrived, Julio's mother explained to me that the police were going to deport her and her boyfriend. "They could come any night now," she said. Almost in tears, she asked if the church could provide her asylum. She said that a friend had told her that it was against the law for the police to come into the church and take them away. Julio gripped his mother's skirt with his small fist.

I repeated what Julio's mother said to the pastor, in English. He shook his head.

"Why not?" I asked.

His gaze was fixed elsewhere, away from us. "The answer is no," he said.

"Please," she said.

"Please," I said.

"I'm sorry," the pastor said, shutting the door.

Julio's mother began to cry. At first she did so softly, and then louder and louder until I was sure that the pastor could hear. Julio cried with her. I tried to help. I asked her if she or a friend knew any lawyers in the area. She nodded defeatedly, in a way that suggested it was too late for a lawyer to help. "Call them," I said, hoping something could still be done. "And if there's a knock at your door, don't open it. Don't say a word."

A year and a half later, this moment still comes back to me every day. Sometimes it comes to me as I try to nap, as I do my best to recover. I think of Julio and his mother when I go for the mail, when I see my neighbors walk to and from the park nearby, when I see their kids play. Yesterday they ran after one another in a screaming game of tag. Today they were still. The heat was high, over 110 degrees, and so they stood laughing in a circle, frying an egg on the cracked Tucson pavement.

I've dreamed of going back in time and letting Julio and his mother into the church myself. Since then, I've also learned that even a church is not safe. ICE would have come for them there all the same. No law said they couldn't.

Before heading back to Magdalena's house that night, I took a marker to the pastor's front door. *You are the war you sleep through*, I wrote.

They let me go a week before Christmas. They had Grace tell me.
"Why?" I asked. "I don't cost much."

MAGDALENA'S BASEMENT

I don't know what I wasn't mourning. I didn't leave the basement for days. I drank little. I ate less. In the mornings, I fried eggs. In the afternoon, I fried eggs. If I had anything in the evenings, I ate a banana or two. I drank milk and I smoked tobacco. Every day brought more news, all of it bad. Trump appointed one Klansman after another to his staff. A big wave was coming. I thought of my mother, father, and sister. I thought of Adriana and João. I thought of Ms. Monti. Of Nico. Of Raúl. What I did most was sleep. I slept poorly. When I dreamed, I dreamed that I was awake.

I became somewhat sick. My head hurt. My neck hurt. My stomach, too. I wanted to perform some grand gesture. I wanted to start over. I thought of changing my name. I considered Nico, João, Adriana, Raúl. Rocío and Tuesday. Like many others, I imagined leaving the country. Colombia might be better, I thought. Or Canada. Maybe Magdalena and I would go to Spain, together. We could go back to Guernica. The United States, the empire, it seemed, was rotting. I thought of Nico.

How he'd grown sicker by the month, the week, the day. I asked myself what he would do. He would continue, for a while. Then he would leave.

I went upstairs when I ran out of my own food. I looked to Magdalena's kitchen and found her in her chair, in front of the television.

"You're alive," she said.

I did what I knew how to do. I began with my own basement. First, I vacuumed the carpet. Then I mopped the kitchen and the bathroom. I swept the stairs. I polished Magdalena's hardwood floors, scrubbed her kitchen, and dusted the blinds. I shined her leather couches, buffed her wooden tables, and renewed her silver. I made her bed and folded her clothes. I bleached her bathroom, bleached her toilet, and scrubbed the mold from the corners of her bathtub. I washed and hung the slip-mats and hung them out to dry in the winter sun. I changed the lightbulbs. I straightened each and every painting in the house.

When I finished, I sat with Magdalena in front of the television. Neither of us spoke. I watched her from across the room, her hands folded in her lap, her head tilted slightly forward. I kept my eyes on hers as the newsman spoke from a parking lot somewhere in Arizona. "Nine illegal aliens were found dead in the back of an abandoned truck," he said. Authorities suspected that there might have been up to one hundred people in the truck before they'd fled. The newscast cut to an interview of the sheriff, taken on scene, in the parking lot of the superstore where the truck, and the bodies, had been found.

"We expect there are more casualties than we've found so far," he said.

When the news was through for the night, Magdalena switched the television to a reality show. The program depicted two eager contestants who challenged themselves to survive in the wild for three weeks, naked, without anything but a knife and a hatchet. The episode was set in the Colombian Amazon. When the three weeks were through, the two contestants returned to their homes, families, and jobs in the United States.

Magdalena asked me to help her up to bed. She kissed me on the cheek before getting into bed. I shut off the light. I was closing the door.

"You weren't wrong," she said.

"About what?" I asked.

"What you wrote," she said. "We are the war we sleep through."

The next morning I took a walk and found that a light snow had dusted the city. The grass in Rose Park was wet with fall's dead leaves. I stayed on the trail and found myself slowed down by a couple and their toddler daughter, who followed closely behind them. They turned several times to see me. I waved. They grabbed their daughter and positioned her in front of them. I stopped and watched them go. The couple turned around again. I waved. I cut across the outfield toward home base. Behind the backstop a lamppost was covered with fliers, most of them expired concerts and fundraisers and talks. Two dogs were missing, a basset hound and a terrier. A third had been found. If I located both dogs I'd be rich. If I found just one I'd be in business.

I followed a set of paw prints for half a mile or so along the edge of the creek. I came to a bridge. The prints trailed off into the water. On the opposite shore, beneath the bridge, a woman sat cross-legged next to a tent. She cast a line with her fishing pole. A basset hound appeared beside her and barked.

"I could get you two thousand dollars for that dog," I said.

"And I could get you deported," she said.

I never knew the difference between an embassy and a consulate. That day I passed plenty of both on my way to a bench across the street from two neighboring offices. The first belonged to an unnamed psychic. The second belonged to a urologist named Alma Chavez. According to what was printed on the window, Alma specialized in state-of-the-art vasectomies. *Vote for Alma*, it read. One middle aged man left the clinic with a slight limp. Twenty minutes later a younger man walked out looking serious and satisfied. I inquired about the procedure. "You're too young for that," they said.

The sign outside the fortune teller's stated that I could get a palm reading for five dollars. I opened the door and was surprised to find nothing more than a family home. An old woman and a young boy sat together on the couch, watching cartoons. A younger woman emerged with a lit cigarette and asked me what I wanted. According to her, the palm reading was ten dollars, cash, and not five.

"Okay," I said.

She sat me down in the corner, surrounded our little table with a curtain, and took my open hand. "You are not from here," she said.

I nodded.

"You have one sibling," she said.

I nodded again.

"You are going to get married once and you are going to have children."

I asked her if my future marriage included a divorce.

"I'll have to read the other palm," she said. "Five dollars more."

I declined her offer and she continued with the initial reading.

"You are going to be successful," she said.

I asked her what that meant.

"Rich," she said.

The last thing she told me was that soon I'd have clarity.

"Clarity?" I asked.

"Yes," she said.

I was counting ten dollars when the boy walked up beside us. He hid behind her. She looked at the boy and asked what was wrong. The boy pointed at me.

"You aren't real," he said.

People continued walking in and out of the vasectomy clinic. In the time I sat there watching, not one person went to the psychic. Most people passed by, not seeming to notice either one and entertain the possibilities. I wondered which business had been there first. I wondered what it would take for a person to end up in these lines of work.

When I got back, Magdalena was putting together a couple of peanut butter and jelly sandwiches. I told her the news. "According to the psychic, I'm going to be a father."

"Congratulations," Magdalena said.

Over lunch, I tried to convince Magdalena my opportunities were good. "Someone will hire me," I insisted. "It only takes one urologist. It only takes one psychic."

"Why don't you take it easy?" Magdalena said.

"Is that allowed?"

"Of course it's allowed."

"What about money?" I asked.

"What *about* money?" Magdalena said.

I never watched more television in my life than I did with Magdalena at the end of that long year. Television, however, is a strong word. We watched movies. We cooked. I cleaned. We drank red wine. We shared a couch. We shared an ashtray.

"I'll quit next year," she laughed.

"Me too," I said.

Magdalena's favorite actor was Gena Rowlands. Her favorite director was John Cassavetes. They were, as she put it, her favorite couple. Gena Rowlands and Magdalena were practically identical. The only real difference between them was that Magdalena's hair was silver and not gold.

Magdalena had first seen Gena Rowlands on screen when she was at university. A boyfriend of hers took her to the cine-club in Madrid that played movies from all over the world. There, she saw *Faces*. "I felt closer to the actors in that movie than I did to most people I'd met, closer than everyone in my life at the time," Magdalena said.

What Magdalena said made sense. The first time I saw *Faces*, the first time I saw Gena Rowlands, I wanted to reach through the screen. I wanted, in some way, to reach through the screen and touch everyone in that movie. After the movie ended, and Magdalena and I had finished our second bottle of wine, I touched her face instead. And she touched mine. And we made love, finally, for the first time.

We were falling asleep, my head resting on her shoulder, my hand in her hair. Magdalena asked if it had been my first time. It hadn't. I told her so.

"What was it like?" she asked.

"I had a girlfriend. I lit candles. We were in the middle of it when her cell phone rang. She answered. Her friend was outside, in my driveway, waiting in a car to take her somewhere. My girlfriend got dressed, kissed me, and left."

Magdalena tried not to laugh, then laughed hard. I did too. She kissed the top of my head.

"It could've been worse," she said.

"What was your first time like?" I asked.

Magdalena didn't answer. Then she snored softly.

We made love every night and some mornings. In between, we watched movies. We watched *Opening Night* and *A Woman Under the Influence*. We watched *Love Streams* and *Gloria*. They all blended together. In a couple of the movies, some guy tells Gena Rowlands to be herself. At least two times, a father gives his young children beer to drink. The same father screams at Gena Rowlands, his wife. Her own father is present. He does not defend her. When she asks him to stand up for her, he proceeds to stand up from his chair, confused. I have, since first watching these movies with Magdalena, re-watched them many times. If I had to choose a favorite scene, I would choose two. The first is the scene when Gena Rowlands' three children come home from school. On the front steps of her house, she begs her children not to get older. The second is the scene when Gena Rowlands asks her brother, after losing her daughter and husband to a divorce, if he thinks love is a kind of art.

Magdalena's favorite part, I learned, was when Gena Rowlands asks if love was a continuous stream.

"Is it?" I asked.

"No."

It was Christmas Eve. We were in Magdalena's bed. We were kissing each other's feet.

"How do you want to celebrate?" Magdalena asked.

"Wine," I said.

"But what to pair it with?"

"Chinatown Express."

"Are they open?"

"They must be."

"And how else should we celebrate? What do you want?" she asked.

I thought of several Christmases with my family, some better than others. I thought of the steak we'd had, the beer and rum and wine we'd drank, the "Little Drummer Boy," and the game we tended to play: Dudo, in Spanish.

"Liars' Dice," I said.

"Ah," Magdalena said, "I know that game well."

"Do you have the cups? Do you have the dice?"

"You worry about the food," she said, "I'll worry about the rest."

I was buttoning my shirt before the mirror, watching Magdalena in our bed behind me.

"I love you, too," she said.

I walked to Chinatown. I stopped at a gift shop a block from the restaurant and bought six lucky cats, each of them gold. The woman at the register was all smiles.

"All for you?" she asked.

"No," I said, "gifts."

"Happy Christmas," she said.

I was surprised to find I wasn't the only one out to eat, even if I was the only person eating alone. I said hello to the boss.

"For here or to go?" he asked.

"Both," I said.

I ordered Peking duck for there. For home, I ordered just about everything on the menu. Seafood and pork dumplings. Pork buns. Spring rolls. Egg rolls. Fried shrimp. Lobster fried rice. Hunan scallops. Pig's belly and soft-shell crab. Twice cooked pork, fresh noodle soup, soy sauce cuttle fish. Intestines.

I watched the chef roll dough at the window below a row of hanging ducks. I thought of what my sister had once said. That there was a dying animal inside each one of us.

The boss brought the duck. Naturally, the fat was the best part. I took my time. Raúl appeared next to me. He refilled my glass of water. *Holy water*, I thought. We spoke in Spanish.

"How are you?" I asked.

"Good," he said. "Thank God."

"Yes," I said. "Thank God."

I opened three fortune cookies on the Metro ride home. The first told me not to depart from the path which fate had assigned me. The second told me that the road to success was often a lonely one. The third advertised a movie featuring cartoon pandas.

I came home to a linen table. To a rudimentary nativity scene, made of wood. To white candles, red wine, and dice in leather cups. To Magdalena dressed in green and jeweled with gold. We toasted. To one another, to Raúl, and to our feast. And we ate and drank and smiled and laughed, at a table for six, with food and wine and cigarettes for six, set for two. We played.

If four begin a game, the game always ends with two. My mother would always lose first. It was a game she hated. Nico, of course, never played. Typically, I would exit second. I had a habit of defaulting to aces, in hopes that the hand would not come back around to me. So many times, I could not get the hand to leave. I was doubted as soon as the round began. I had a habit of losing several hands in a row, all my dice gone consecutively, all in a pile, with my mother's, at the center of the table. I won the occasional game. After winning a game I would always go on to lose the next one. As one should, I believe. Most games ended with my sister and father, one-on-one. Although for them, they liked to say, one-on-one was when the game truly began. From there the game would turn into a certain kind of staring contest, one where they both would laugh, slyly, unable to contain their competitive joy. They loved to beat one another as much as they loved anything else. It was an even match. Both won plenty.

I want to say I never gambled. What I can say is that I never gambled money. But we all gamble something more, something much more, than money. Every day. And if not every day, every Christmas. I've never gambled more than I gambled that year. I made a home with Magdalena. I made a God out of one good man.

We began our game the way most games end. Two players, one on one. Magdalena was excellent at lying. She made her living with kings, leaving me little option but to up the number and change the suit, to jacks or queens, or resort, as I always had, to aces. Winning was not enough for Magdalena. We played for little favors. "Loser fetches, opens, and pours the next bottle." I lost and did what I would've happily done had I won. "Loser microwaves the pork buns and dumplings." I lost, quickly, and kept my end of the deal. "Loser tosses the lobster fried rice and soft-shell crab in the pan." Magdalena, it seemed, was fonder of relishing her upper hand than of finishing off a game. The happiest I'd seen her that night, maybe the happiest I'd ever seen her, was when she was up five dice to one. I lost, then cooked. "Loser does the dishes." I did the dishes.

We were at the end of a third bottle, at the end of the night. The dishes were clean. The leftovers were in the refrigerator. "One more game," Magdalena said.

"What are we playing for?" I asked.

"The house," Magdalena said.

We played for the house. I was up two dice to Magdalena's one and still found a way to lose. I started each of the last two games with red tens. Two weak hands played poorly.

"This house is your house," I said.

She laughed. "Maybe next year, Gregorio."

That night, that Christmas, I learned that Magdalena's house would never be my home. Where I belonged was in Magdalena's basement.

Magdalena came downstairs without knocking. I was at the basement desk. "Are you coming upstairs?" she asked.

"I'm going to stay here," I said.

"Alone?"

"No," I said.

Magdalena laughed, stopped laughing, then nodded. She stood behind me, over me, and looked at the postcards before me. "Have you ever written a letter?" she asked.

"Not a real one," I said. "Nico left me one when he was going to die. He talked about letters, once. He said to write a real one, you must be sorry."

"What are you sorry for?" she asked.

"That's what I'm trying to figure out."

Magdalena nodded. She touched the pads of her long fingers to her lips, then spoke through them. "I wrote a few letters once. For my family. But I never sent them."

"Why not?" I asked.

"They were dead," she said.

BATHWATER

For Christmas, I gave Magdalena one of the six lucky cats. She set the gold cat on the table in front of her and stared at it. "It's alive," she said. She handed me a prepaid debit card. The card was worth as much as a missing dog.

It was a cold week to end the year, and yet it felt like the world outside Magdalena's house was burning. Magdalena didn't want me to leave the house. She worried something would happen to me. "They are coming out of the shadows," she said. I knew who she was talking about. I, too, was afraid. The walls were closing in, so to speak, but the house was warm.

We ate soup. Onion, asparagus, squash. We watched a movie each day, sometimes two, wrapped in the same blanket. The days were short. The nights were short, too. We drank in bed, made love in bed, smoked in bed, and fell asleep early. We slept well. We slept late into the mornings, even into the occasional afternoon. We took baths. I would wash every inch of her. Her silver hair. The soles of her feet.

The last day of the year was the coldest. Magdalena and I stood together, in robes, watching hot water run into the tub.

It was up to our ankles when we realized we needed more wine. I ran down to the kitchen for more. The last thing Magdalena said, "Don't forget to come back."

I found her face-down in a foot of bathwater. I pulled her up, by the shoulders, and stopped the faucet. Blood dripped from her silver hair. "Magdalena," I said. "Wake up." I called an ambulance. She was breathing. Poorly, but breathing. I drained the water. She couldn't even shiver.

"Come back," I said. "Come back."

I wasn't Magdalena's husband and I wasn't family. I was her tenant. I provided her name and address to the hospital. This was what I could do. The doctor could not, would not, tell me much of anything. "She's alive," she said. The way she said so, with a certain silence, told me everything. It would have been better if Magdalena had died.

In the waiting room, there were more people than chairs. I sat in a corner on the tile floor. At best, I thought, a coma is a prayer. I thought of Nico's death. I wondered if I was a curse. I imagined a future in which I would avoid growing too close to anyone. It wouldn't be a normal life, but it would be a common one. I wondered, too, if I was some type of shepherd, my purpose being to help the living die. I wanted to tell this to someone. I wanted to tell Magdalena.

I was smoking in a designated area. A nurse was with me, taking a break. "It's the busiest night of the year," he said. "Busier than Christmas." Later, the same nurse woke me up. I was asleep in my corner of the waiting room. He brought me a pillow and a warm blanket.

"Any news?" I asked.

"She's still alive," he said.

Death, it turned out, was normal.

I woke up before sunrise. The janitor was mopping the floor around me. I looked up at him.

"I'm sorry," I said, standing up to make room.

He nodded. "Happy New Year," he said.

It took me an hour to eat my plate of cafeteria eggs, and another hour to eat my cafeteria sandwich. Everyone there ate at a similar pace, like farm animals grazing.

When I returned to the waiting room, I was told that someone would like to speak with me. I figured there was news, that Magdalena had finally fallen asleep for good. A woman in a blue suit approached me. Her hair was long and blond, and she was wearing large white pearls around her neck. For a moment, I thought it was Magdalena. A new Magdalena. Some sort of miracle. She held her hand out to me.

"Gregorio," she said, "my name is June Fee."

June Fee was Magdalena's younger sister, her only sibling, the only direct family Magdalena had left. The hospital had managed to contact June upon Magdalena's arrival. June boarded an immediate train to D.C. from Connecticut. She did not cry when she spoke with me. It didn't seem as if she'd cried at all. Still, she managed to be kind.

"But Magdalena is an orphan," I said.

"That's the story she told," June said.

According to June, Magdalena had been born Helen Fee. She was neither Basque nor an orphan. Helen had been born to two parents in a large home in a small town. They'd grown up where they'd been born, in Pluto, Connecticut. A few towns over from Danbury. Helen left home at sixteen. Why, June couldn't, or wouldn't, say. When, how, and why Helen became Magdalena, June couldn't, or wouldn't, say either.

Their father died first. For that funeral, Magdalena did not appear. Years later, Magdalena appeared at her mother's small service. It was the first time June had seen her sister since she'd left, decades before.

"What was it like?" I asked.

June reached into her purse. She pulled out a piece of gum, unwrapped it, and dropped it into her mouth. She looked around the waiting room as she chewed, as if she were chewing the very words she was choosing not to tell me.

"She was another person. Somehow, she was better."

Thanks to June, I saw Helen. I pressed my head to her head. I kissed the palms of her hands.

"Helen," I said.

I failed to weep. In a way it felt like Magdalena hadn't died. It felt like she'd never really existed. A soreness came over me, then numbness.

I walked a straight line to Chinatown Express. It was still morning when I arrived, and they weren't yet open for the day. Through the window I saw the boss sitting alone at a table by the counter. He had his glasses on and a big calculator in his hands. He was going through a large pile of receipts. I opened the door and said hello. He looked up at me and removed his glasses. "Can I help you?" he asked. I told him that I wanted to work. I told him I would do whatever was asked of me.

"What's your name?" he asked.

"Gregorio Pasos."

GOALKEEPING

June made it clear I was free to stay, in the basement, "For the time being." She stayed at a hotel nearby, leaving the house empty. Magdalena's death was an imminent fact. The doctors made it clear to June and June made it clear to me. I didn't know who, or how, to mourn. There was a part of me that believed Magdalena could still make it back. Every night she was in the hospital, I pictured her return home. I dreamed we would sit together in the kitchen, again. I'd ask her about Helen.

Raúl taught me how to keep up. We washed dishes, mopped floors, bussed tables, and handed out menus. He showed me the correct way to walk around a corner, and most importantly, what to say and where to stand. My quick development resulted in Raúl's promotion. He began rolling dough, folding dumplings, and waiting on the occasional table.

Raúl invited me to play soccer with a group of his friends. His friends turned out to be many, and what I had imagined would be a casual kick-around ended up being an adult league game. I volunteered to play goalkeeper and was thanked for doing so.

No one else wanted to occupy the net, which made sense. It was cold and running was easier than standing still. That, and there was more to lose than there was to gain.

Raúl played left-back. He ran all night, up and down his sideline, always making himself available for a teammate in attack, or a teammate in trouble. He played smooth crosses to the taller forwards when the looks were good, but never hesitated to put his foot on the ball, pass back to one of the center-backs, and start over. When he played a bad pass, he tracked back on defense, quickly and calmly. But he rarely played a poor pass, and he never forced anything. And most importantly, when I was playing the ball out, he was always there to receive it.

At work, they called me Pasos. When we played soccer, they called me Portero.

That was my name over the course of that tenure. Keeper in English. A brotherly term. Portero in Spanish meant something else entirely. Guard. Doorman. Watchman. Raúl called me both, dependent on the company we were in.

It was the best season of my life. I played with Raúl, and I played well. Well enough, that is, for the team to win all but one of its weekly games. My job was simply not to mess up. If I didn't make a mistake, or too many mistakes, everything would be fine.

This was not any kind of official league. Uniforms were optional and a consistent color was good enough. Our team wore green. Raúl and several of the other players wore different iterations of the same Mexican national team jersey. Raúl played without a name and without a number. I did too. As a goalkeeper, I could wear what I wanted, so long as it wasn't the same color as the opponent, and so long as it wasn't green.

The games were organized, though, as was the league. A reasonably small fee was necessary to reserve time slots for the shotty fields where we played, and to pay the eager referees who loved to hear the sound of their own whistles. It was said to me by an opponent, prior to a corner kick being taken, that we were the most carded team in the division, that we didn't play the right way. The score was 3-0 at the time, in my team's favor. Every player on the other team wore the same new uniforms with royal blue justice scales as logos. A team of law students, it seemed, or worse, barred lawyers. The specific opponent who said this about my team, a very blond man with very bright eyes, said so in a way that indicated he'd never been on the losing side of anything without an excuse. I didn't say anything. For the rest of the game, I studied the way he played. He was a central midfielder who liked to demand the ball. He played all of his passes forward. He never played them backward. He never played them sideways.

Raúl was the most yellow-carded player on the team. He picked one up every game. But, unlike some of our other teammates, he never saw a red. I never worried he would, either. It's been said that knowing how to defend is knowing how to foul. By this metric, Raúl was the best defender I've ever known. His infractions were not acts of frustration, aggression, or retaliation. They were simply correct decisions. Like the sly tug of a forward's shirt during a counterattack, or a subtle trip of an opponent running full speed. If he were to commit a desperate foul, where he'd clearly been beat, he always did so outside the penalty box, and sometimes on the very edge of it, on the line. He wasn't always in exactly the right place, but he always knew where he was. That, and where he needed to be.

Before games, Raúl would practice taking penalties, and therefore I would practice trying to save them. Many, if not all of the coaches I'd ever had would have disagreed with Raúl's approach. He aimed his penalties high, toward the crossbar. Ideally, penalties should be aimed low. The assumption is that nerves cause penalty takers to lean backward when they should otherwise stand over the ball when striking, causing them to sail the ball over the goal. The worst thing a penalty taker can do is miss. Many penalty takers focus on the goalkeeper, on reading which way the goalie is going to dive, which way the goalie is going to guess, and simply pass the ball into the empty side of the net. In a way, Raúl was the opposite. He took penalties as if there were no goalkeeper at all.

I was enjoying a shower before work when the phone rang upstairs. I ignored it. It rang again while I was drying off. I got dressed. The phone started a third time. I answered. It was June Fee.

"I have news," she said.

"Good or bad?" I asked.

"Both," she said.

"Give me the bad news first," I said.

"Helen passed away last night."

"What's the good news?" I asked.

"That is the good news," she said.

I made my way to work. *Magdalena's dead,* I thought, *Magdalena was never born.* I wept as I walked. Privately, the way one should, among others, as part of a larger commute. With one hand in each pocket, a cold nose, and short strides.

That day I worked the corner. I did my best to stand still. I held the stack of menus in one arm and a single menu in my other hand. There were no protesters and few tourists. The *Good News from God* folks were there, smiling. Snot froze on my top lip. My arms got tired. My legs did too.

Raúl stopped by with two cups of tea. I set the stack of menus down and offered him a cigarette. "I don't smoke," he said, "I quit."

"How?" I asked.

"I stopped," he said.

"When?" I asked.

"Which time?" he laughed.

Raúl explained that he used to stop smoking for every soccer season. When he would stop he would dream about smoking, happy dreams where he would try to stay asleep and smoke as much as possible. But now his soccer seasons were constant. Added up, his soccer seasons, all four of them, almost equaled a year.

I asked him about next season, and if I was welcome to play again.

"Of course," he said. "But I probably won't be here."

"Where are you going?" I asked.

"Hermosillo, Sonora, Mexico," he said.

"Home?"

He nodded. "My mother," he said, tilting his head, implying the worst.

"How long has it been since you've seen her?" I asked.

"Years," he said.

I was washing dishes at the end of our shift when Raúl walked into the kitchen, singing a corrido. A few of the cooks joined in. I sang with them the way everyone sings a song they don't know, predicting every sixth word and merging into the longer notes.

That night, the last game before the playoffs, we won 5-0. If the team had played without me the score would've been the same. I only touched the ball two or three times, when Raúl would pass it back to me. He laughed when he did so. "So you don't get bored!" he called.

I remember thinking of Raúl and his mother. I imagined him returning home, to a small house in a small city in the desert, with brothers and sisters and dogs there to greet him. In that moment, at the edge of the penalty box, I felt with real certainty that I knew where everyone was. My father, in Nico's house, with a drink in hand, asleep or awake, in front of a television. My sister, somewhere in Arizona, doing the same. And my mother, somewhere in Santa Marta, sitting upright in bed next to my grandmother, listening to the nightly Mass on an old radio at full volume. I knew where everyone was and I didn't know how to get to them. And I'm not sure if I wanted to, either. What I wanted was for someone, any one of them, all of them, to find me. I've learned that this is a common want. I've learned that most wants are common.

The next morning, I woke up to June Fee knocking at the front door. I was soon after informed that Magdalena's house, the house on whose door June had just spent five minutes knocking, now belonged to her. That was no surprise. I expected her to ask for my keys, or to declare a date by which I had to move out, but she didn't.

"What are you going to do with the house?" I asked.

"I don't know," she said.

"You could keep it. You could rent it. You could sell it," I said.

June laughed as if she hadn't laughed in months. "We'll see," she said. She declined to have breakfast but accepted black tea. "Helen left you something," she said. I looked at June. A letter, I thought. Or a movie.

"What?" I asked.

"Money," June said.

"For what?" I said.

June showed me the will. There, in bolded ink, was my legal name and my description. "My Beloved Tenant." Magdalena left me more money than I would've made in a decade working at Chinatown Express, more than I would've saved working that way for the rest of my life.

"What are you going to do with the money?" June asked.

"No idea," I said.

June grinned. "You could save it. You could spend it. You could invest it."

I was late for work. At the door, I said goodbye to June.

"Goodbye, beloved tenant," she said.

Raúl was on the corner, holding the menus I was supposed to be handing out. "Portero," he said. "You're late."

Of the sixteen teams in our recreational soccer league, eight made the playoffs. We were one of them. We won our first game by a goal. We went down 2-0. The first goal came from a corner. I stayed on my line when I should've come out to meet the cross. The second goal was a penalty. I guessed the wrong way. Raúl cut their lead to one with a nice cross to our best forward. Then we tied the game from a breakaway chance. Finally, Raúl converted an easy penalty, right under the crossbar, with only a minute left in regulation time.

I was about to head off to the Metro station when Raúl called me back over to the bench. He was with his wife. He was holding their daughter. "Portero," he said, "this is my wife. This is my daughter." I shook hands with the woman and then with the girl.

"Get home safe," I said.

"If God wants," Raúl said.

The day of the quarterfinal, Raúl brought some hot tea to the corner to share during his break. We talked about the previous game and how much better we could've, and should've, played.

"Maybe we'll win," he said. "Maybe we'll lose. All we can do is play well."

Raúl said the same thing to the whole team before each game. It was usually met with a combination of disregard and laughter. Disregard because winning, over the course of the season, had become a foregone conclusion. Laughter because what Raúl said was true. I tended to laugh.

I asked Raúl if his wife and daughter were going to be at the game. He said yes. I also asked if they'd be with him when he went back home. "Maybe they'll come," he said. "Maybe they'll stay."

Referees are, for some reason, necessary. This is true even when there's nothing much at stake. In our little league, the referee was responsible for keeping score and for keeping games, and therefore tensions, civil. What was uncommon about our referees was that they were also tasked with painting the lines. Sidelines, endlines, penalty areas, goal lines. Typically, they arrived early to do so. The lines were never perfectly straight. It's impossible to paint a perfectly straight line. And it's hard to draw a good one. And there's always something at stake.

That night the referee arrived late, ten minutes after the game was scheduled to begin. He painted the lines quickly and poorly, especially making a mess of the goal line. I asked him if he didn't think the line was a problem. He shook his head. I asked him if he heard me. "I heard you," he said. Up until that game, I'd never said anything to a referee other than thank you.

There are many games that seem destined to end in a tie. It doesn't matter how good and disciplined and organized either side plays. The quarterfinal was that kind of game. We had our chances, good ones, but that's all they were. They had theirs, too. But a quarterfinal can't end in a tie, and therefore ends with penalties.

Penalties are easy to make. That's what makes them hard. Both teams stand at half-field, watching in silence. Both goalkeepers take turns in net. The penalty taker places the ball on the spot, waits for the referee to blow the whistle, then shoots. When my team was shooting, I stood to the side, on the endline, watching.

I saved the first penalty. It was poorly taken, but I stopped it. I guessed right and caught the shot. It was the first penalty I'd ever saved, but it wasn't enough. Our team missed the first penalty, too. We also missed the last. Raúl took it. I'd never seen such a perfect penalty. He took it calmly, as if there were no goalkeeper, as if no one else was watching, as if there was no one else in the world. He struck the ball cleanly down the middle. The goalie dove aggressively to one side and watched the ball as he fell to the dirt. The ball hit the crossbar and then shot downward, clearing the awfully drawn line. The spin caused it to bounce upward off the ground and out of the goal. It's the referee's job to watch the ball, and the line, closely. But the referee said, "No goal."

I don't know if the referee didn't see, or if he chose not to. That's what I asked him, again and again. The other team ran to their goalkeeper to celebrate. Their friends and family joined them on the field. The referee ignored me. I followed him as players from the other team, and a few from ours, politely shook his hand, thanking him. The more he ignored me, the more I raised my voice. I called him every name I could think of. He didn't even look at me. I felt the players from both teams inching closer to intervene. I heard someone mention the police. I kept going. I stood over the referee as he tucked his whistle into his backpack, as he changed out of his cleats and into sneakers. That's when Raúl put himself between us. He pushed me slowly and firmly away, repeating himself. "It doesn't matter, Gregorio. This doesn't matter."

TUCSON

These days are as short as ever. All they do is pass along. And yet, with each one, I remember more. Two weeks have passed since I broke my ribs. It hurts to move, but everyday there's less pain than the day before. I can laugh without a problem. My appetite has returned. I can eat all I want. I've quit smoking and still I'm short of breath. The medication continues to bring me fog and nausea, even in low doses. Some nights it's difficult to fall asleep. I get overwhelmed with visions of what I could have done differently. This I've learned. I wish I'd moved in with Nico sooner. I wish I had slip-proofed Magdalena's bathtub. I wish I'd saved every penalty I ever faced.

I no longer eat eggs. Meat either. I haven't had a drink in weeks. I take my vitamins. B-12, iron, magnesium. I'm working on my posture. Once a day, I sit straight against the wall and stretch my arms upward. Ramona says I look better. Healthier. "That's because I am," I say.

Ramona's been reading a book about how to talk to plants. "They know what we're feeling," she says. "They can hear everything. Each part of them can see light."

The other night, Ana joined Ramona and me for dinner. Before eating, we sat out on the back porch for an hour or so while my sister rolled one spliff after another and updated us on her job. One of her two missing clients was recently located and returned to the area. He's now living with his cousin in Phoenix as he awaits his trial. There's no news from the other. Her caseload has grown on account of yet another attorney, the second in three months, leaving the nonprofit organization she works for. Despite the organization's reputation, they exploit their workers. The plan, as of now, is to unionize. Ana is optimistic. The conversation ends with my sister's favorite anecdote about a new client she's particularly fond of. The charge working against his case for legal residency in the United States is an old grand theft auto conviction. According to the police, he stole a horse.

Over dinner—white rice with jackfruit, avocado, and beans—we discussed Ramona's project at Tumamoc Hill and the nature of my recovery, both of which, we reported, are going well enough.

Before leaving, my sister insisted we watch a short documentary a coworker had recommended. *Paraíso.* The movie profiles three window washers in downtown Chicago. Each day, they rappel from the roof of a given skyscraper and clean the glass buildings. They describe the worlds they peer into each day on the job: rich old women with expensive jewelry, young men getting drunk together, the occasional couple having sex. The profession, of course, is often fatal. The documentarian asks them what they believe will happen to them after they die. One of the washers says you end up in a drawer. Another says you go to another world, one where you're alone in your own paradise.

There's a lizard in our house. When I first noticed it, I opened the door to let it out. But it wouldn't leave. It likes to lean over the bottom rail of the sliding glass door and look into the garden. I set out a small bowl of water and refill it daily. The lizard eats the crickets that find their way into the walls. The crickets used to keep Ramona and me up at night. Last night, the house was quiet as a church.

This morning I went for a walk, my first time leaving the house since arriving home from the hospital. I walked slowly. The neighborhood lacked its usual peace. I passed more people than I'd ever remembered passing. I didn't recognize anyone. I heard tires screeching from the main street, and a steady stream of shouts. I walked over. Two patrol cars blocked traffic from entering. A few trailers were set up around the perimeter of the block. Everyone seemed, at once, frantic, in control, and guided by some small and significant sense of duty.

I decided to stop by the corner market for a cup of coffee. A cop in sunglasses asked me for my credentials. I told him I was late for work at the corner market. He asked me for proof. I told him I didn't have proof. We looked at one another for a moment. "I'm late," I said. Finally, he let me pass, so long as I understood not to interrupt the shoot.

The corner store's windows, I noticed, were dirty. The coffee was fresh and bitter and required milk to enjoy. I asked María, the owner, if she knew what was being filmed.

"A Western," she said.

"Good for business?" I asked.

María laughed. "Incredible."

Outside, I watched the film crew prepare the set for another take. The scene went like this. The protagonist—handsome, bearded, and blond—wears tan leather boots and a matching holster on his hip. With a pistol in one hand, he slides frantically into the driver's seat of an old red mustang and slams the door.

He speeds off, then slams the breaks at the end of the block. Two clouds of dust remain; one where he started, and another where he ended. No one, it appeared, had ever been after him.

My hospital bill arrived in the mail. It turns out I owe them three thousand dollars. The first thing I thought of was how I was going to fight the cost. The second thing I thought of was Magdalena and the money she left me, her beloved tenant.

I call Raúl. He's still in Mexico, in Hermosillo, with his family. They live there now and have no immediate plans to return. His mother passed away a few days ago, and the funeral is the day after tomorrow.

"Why don't you come?" he says. "If you can."

"Of course I can," I say. "I'll be there."

I cleaned our house the other day. I even polished the windows. I wish I hadn't. A clean house, I've learned, has a cost. The cleaner the windows are, the more likely a mourning dove is to fly into them. Every day a dove crashes. Sometimes two. I bury them in our small yard, one next to the other. I do so in the evenings when the world is still. When the sky is purple. When the mourning doves, those still living, sing their common song.

ACKNOWLEDGMENTS

I would like to thank the people who have influenced the writing of this book over the years. Their insight, encouragement, support, and friendship have been fundamental to the realization of this project. Their ways of living, thinking, teaching, working, and writing have changed me for the better.

Many thanks to Derrick Austin, Amy Quan Barry, Rebecca Bedell, Oliver Baez Bendorf, Sean Bishop, Jamel Brinkley, Vickie Caicedo, Leila Chatti, Jo Blair Cipriano, Tiana Clark, Maddy Court, Rodrigo Duran, Natalie Eilbert, Adrian Evans, Marta Evans, Danielle Evans, Gonzalo Mallarino Flórez, Sarah Fuchs, Marcela Fuentes, Christopher J. Greggs, Mark Haber, Rebekah Hewitt, Alexis Sears, Jordan Jacks, Amaud Jamaul Johnson, Josh Kalscheur, Jesse Lee Kercheval, Kabel Mishka Ligot, Gary Lovely, Juan Merino, Judith Claire Mitchell, Saretta Morgan, Sean Patrick Mulroy, Jamil Nayani, Jack Ortiz, Lisa Page, Leslie Sainz, Carrie Schuettpelz, Jennie Seidewand, Tariq Shah, Emily Shetler, Barrett Swanson, Isaac Testa, Dylan Weir, and Javier Zamora.

Thank you to *Joyland Magazine*, *Triangle House Review*, *X-R-A-Y*, and *SPECTRA* for selecting, editing, publishing, and promoting my work. And to The University of Wisconsin-Madison Graduate Program in Creative Writing for the gifts of time, funding, and community.

I'm especially thankful to Eric Obenauf and Eliza Wood-Obenauf for their belief in this project, their invaluable editorial guidance, and for giving my work the perfect home. I'm so happy to have worked on this book together. Thanks, also, to Brett Gregory and everyone at Two Dollar Radio for their support.

This book was helped along thanks to the guidance and encouragement of my beloved mentors, readers, and friends. Thank you Alyssa Asquith, H.G. Carrillo / Herman Glenn Carroll, Tia Clark, Wes Holtermann, Edward P. Jones, Ron Kuka, Judith Claire Mitchell, Melissa Mogollón, and Dantiel W. Moniz.

I could not have written this without the love of my family. Thanks to my mother, Olga. My father, Sergio. My sister, Valentina. And my life partner, Morgan.

Thank you, everyone, for everything. See you around.